The JASMINE Portfolio

Fiona Beddow is an ex-musician, teacher and author who writes adventure novels. When she is not hunched over a computer keyboard typing with four fingers, she works as a home tutor, specialising in helping children with special needs and building confidence in numeracy and literacy skills. She gives writing workshops with a musical twist, and talks to children about the adventure of writing. She is an advocate for the rights and aspirations of girls around the world.

ISBN-10: 1502489473
ISBN-13: 978-1502489470

Cover design: Spiffing Covers

**Follow Fiona on Twitter
@FionaBeddow**

www.fionabeddowbooks.com

The JASMINE Portfolio

Fiona Beddow

Also by Fiona Beddow:

Fierce Resistance

The JASMINE Portfolio

PROLOGUE

The doors of the community hall swung open and the women surged in. Like spiders on a web, they scuttled to the tables in the middle of the room in search of plunder.

The SUPPORT charity workers had laid out the linen beautifully. Luxury duvet covers and sheets, immaculately sealed in smooth, clear plastic. Pure Egyptian cotton and lace, donated by an exclusive department store to help families in need.

'What do you call this?' scoffed a woman with long, pearl-encrusted fingernails. 'Nothing goes together! Where's the pillow cases for this cover?'

A charity worker explained that the linen was all 'end of line' and that not everything would match. The woman drummed her false nails on the table, her eyes narrowing. Then she tossed back her head and spat on the floor.

A howl of discontent spread through the group. The women mauled the bedclothes, searching for matching items and baying with anger when nothing could be found. There was a ripping sound: fingernail woman plunged her stiletto heel into a sheet and tore it apart from top to bottom. As the charity workers stood helplessly, handbags were unzipped and scissors, tweezers and nail files stabbed the fine cloth and pulled it to shreds. Somebody took out their phone and made a call.

Ten minutes later, two men arrived carrying petrol cans, and the SUPPORT workers fled through the back of the building. The women threw the bed linen into a pile; the men doused it with fuel and set it alight. Soon afterwards, as the protesters chanted in the street outside, a pack of journalists arrived – and then the fire service, who extinguished the flames before they engulfed the building. The police arrived and watched from a distance.

Another phone call was made and, half an hour later, a limousine with tinted windows pulled up. The chauffeur got out and opened the rear passenger door. A pair of elegant legs wearing sheer black stockings slid sideways, and shiny leather shoes clicked onto the pavement. A woman in a sharp suit and Gucci sunglasses got out and walked towards the press, shouting into her phone. From the other side of the limo strode a dark-haired man, his grey eyes the only hint of colour against his black suit and polo shirt. He joined his wife in front of the bank of cameras.

'I am sure we don't need any introduction,' he said. 'But in case you don't know who we are, this is Flick Stryder and my name is Julian Jones.'

The camera shutters whirred in a frenzy.

'This situation is an absolute disgrace,' said Ms Stryder, as a video camera broadcasted the interview live on TV. '*Nobody* should have to sleep under bedclothes that aren't properly co-ordinated.'

Julian Jones agreed. 'First the soup kitchens were only providing a choice of three soups, and now this. It's inhumane.'

Stryder beckoned to fingernail woman to join her, hissing a reminder in her ear that she should let her lawyer do the talking. 'We will be representing the Better Bedcover Movement in court. The people at SUPPORT *will* pay for this injustice.'

The cameras clicked again and the reporters shouted questions, but the Stryder-Joneses ignored them all. They returned to their car and it sped away with a whoosh of tyres on the tarmac.

The TV news camera continued to roll, and a reporter stepped in front of the lens.

'No doubt the government will be looking into this,' she said. 'But with the formidable Stryder-Joneses leading the campaign for compensation, it will only be a matter of time before the Prime Minister decides to back the protesters. SUPPORT will *not* be 'supported'.'

Fingernail woman smiled. She stepped forward to be interviewed, her gold fillings, expensive falsies and the screen of her smartphone glinting brightly in the spring sunshine.

I

Jac Stryder-Jones wasn't the sort of girl to get squeamish about a bit of dirt. But the stench coming from the protest camp was disgusting.

Every Monday to Friday she zigzagged through the patchwork of tents, watched by anonymous protesters - their eyeballs twitching behind plastic pig masks. Each day, a mush of sights, sounds and smells encircled her: vibrant, embroidered banners and exotic pavement art; folk music colliding with reggae colliding with Mozart colliding with whale-song; incense fumes mixed with all-day Balti, coffee and chips. And riding over the top of this multi-sensory bombardment was the overpowering stink of forgotten rubbish bags left in unoccupied tents.

An egg struck her on the shoulder and yolk oozed down the sleeve of her blazer.

'Private school scum!'

A pig-faced protester threw a second egg and it hit her school hat. Jac picked off the eggshell as she walked. She didn't look back. It wasn't her fault her horrible parents were rich enough to send her to one of the best schools in London.

A third egg smashed and dribbled down her back.

'Spoilt little rich girl!'

The protester was wearing a T-shirt that said '*Kiss Me - I'm Too Poor to Buy You Flowers*'. Jac pursed her lips, and pretended to read the slogan:

'Nice shirt! '*Kick ... me ... I'm ... too ... stupid ... to ... notice*' ...'

The protester's eyes blazed. He took a couple of steps forward and clenched his fists.

'Ooh, I'm *soo* scared,' said Jac. She swivelled on her heels and left the camp behind her.

The school gates were soon in sight, a security guard waiting to let Jac in. She stepped off the kerb to cross the road, but the screeching of tyres on the tarmac made her jump back.

A huge truck thundered past in a cloud of dust. A crowd of people stood inside a cage at the back. Their faces were spookily whitened with talc, their teeth and eyeballs glaring yellow. Somebody was shouting through a megaphone; others threw bright orange leaflets into the street.

Jac picked one up. It read:

ARE **YOU** TRAPPED IN **POOL POVERTY**?
We believe everyone has the right to own a
Jacuzzi pool
JOIN OUR CAMPAIGN TO HAVE A
POOL ALLOWANCE INCLUDED IN
BENEFIT PAYMENTS
follow us on dinkytalk @poolprisoners

The lorry disappeared in a cloud of dirt, and there was a moment of calm. Then a fleet of motorcycles sped into the street, the leather-clad pillion passengers throwing handbills into the air. They chased after the lorry, pieces of paper and exhaust fumes streaming behind them.

One of the sheets fluttered down within reach and Jac caught it.

- CHRISTIANS AGAINST POVERTY -
PRAY YOURSELF RICH
WE ARE ON BEST*FRIENDS - PLEASE JOIN US

Jac pushed both leaflets into her school bag and crossed the road. She showed her pass to the security guard, and walked through the electronic scanner into the school grounds.

St. Philomena's School towered above her. She jumped over the 'Keep off the Grass' sign and strode across the lawn to the Year Ten block. After she had hung her blazer and hat in the cloakroom she walked to her classroom and sat down next to Fabian.

'You've got egg in your hair again,' he said, threading his ebony-coloured fingers through her artificially dark curls. 'Gothic Black suits you, by the way. Goes with your eyes.'

'Oh, yuck! Somebody find a bucket so I can puke!'

Rufus Barton appeared like a ghost next to Fabian. He tossed his head back with a sneer. 'Looks like Fabian Traves wants to be a hairdresser when he grows up!' he said. 'What on earth would Daddy have to say about that?'

Jac rolled her eyes. Fabian's dad was the Home Secretary, and Rufus's dad was a top civil servant for the Opposition party. 'Fabian's dad's too busy wiping the floor with your dad,' said Jac.

'That's what *he* thinks,' smirked Rufus.

Fabian ignored him. 'You coming to watch my rehearsal tonight, sweet pea?'

'Sorry – Journalism Club's been moved,' said Jac.

'I won't see you till the performance now.'

'Shame. My Julius Caesar is an *absolute* triumph,' said Fabian with a grin.

'O-M-G! You are *so* gay!' said Rufus.

Fabian said nothing. He got out an exercise book and pretended to check his homework. Jac, however, took her fountain pen, unscrewed the base and squirted it at Rufus, landing a jet of blue ink on his shirt and spattering the dregs all over his face.

'I'll get you back for that!'

'Shut your face, Smurf-boy,' said Jac.

Everybody laughed, and then a deep, booming voice cut across the classroom. It was Mr Figgis, the form tutor.

'Good morning, Jacqueline. I'm pleased to see you enjoy modern art,' he said, staring at the splurge of blue sweeping across Rufus's cheeks. 'So I look forward to reading your essay about it.' He twiddled his moustache. 'The essay you will write during detention this evening.'

Rufus could not conceal his triumph, but his self-congratulation was wasted on Jac. She pulled her jumper up over her mouth to conceal a snigger. She looked at Fabian, whose shoulders bounced silently with laughter. Rufus was going to look like a goof all day. That would be worth a hundred detentions.

When the bell went at four o'clock she threw everything into her bag and went to the detention room. She signed in, then told the teaching assistant she needed to go to the toilet. She walked down two flights of stairs, ran through the cloakroom and out through the fire exit, crossed the car park and entered the humanities block. She took the staff-only lift to the top floor, strode along the corridor and arrived five minutes early for Journalism Club.

'Come in, Jacqueline,' said Miss Steele, looking at her watch. 'Wow! I wish everyone had an attitude like yours.'

Jac took her seat at the front of the class and smiled.

II

Miss Steele brushed a short, red-brown hair from the front of her suit and pressed 'ENTER' on her laptop. The words:

SEEK IT OUT AND SHOUT!

appeared on the whiteboard at the front of the room.

'Short and sweet, huh?' she said, in her strong Chicago accent. She leant back in her chair and crossed her ankles. 'These words are the beating heart of journalism. We sniff out a story, we tell the world what we know. And we do it with a bang.'

She uncrossed her legs with an elegant kick, stood up and paced between the students. 'We write – we challenge – we inspire.' She adjusted her designer spectacles. 'So, what has inspired you this week? Homework, please.'

Jac took out her notes on the North London Urban Farm. She read the opening sentence and thought how dull it was. She didn't really care about the donkeys and the rabbits, or the children who would miss out if it closed. Frustrated, she screwed the paper into a ball and lobbed her work into the waste paper basket.

She searched in her bag and found the two campaign leaflets she had picked up that morning, and laid them side by side. Then she drafted some headlines on a fresh sheet of paper:

Do-Gooders Versus Go-Getters: Britain's Propaganda Battle Heats Up

Is the Middle Class Lifestyle a God-Given Right?

God-Squad Bikers Drive Home Their Message

She stopped and chewed her pen.

'I saw what you did there, Jacqueline.' Miss Steele touched Jac on the shoulder, and pointed towards the scrunched-up paper in the rubbish bin. 'Well done. Sometimes you gotta throw away the old and cause a splash with something new.' She leant closer. 'May I?'

Jac showed her the leaflets.

'These are the start of a great story,' said Miss Steele. 'But don't stop there. Make it bold. Remember: this story found you. And who knows what else has inspired you today without you even noticing?'

She stood up and straightened her glasses. 'Dig deep. Don't be afraid to go to places you never thought you'd go.'

Jac scribbled down more headlines, her heart pumping:

What Would Jesus Do? Judge or Forgive?

Why Does Everyone Hate Everybody Else?

No. They were worse than the first lot. She closed her eyes and breathed in the last atoms of Miss Steele's perfume as it faded to a dusky haze.

Without warning, her thoughts jumped backwards in time and once again she was walking through the protest camp. A foul combination of smells re-entered her nostrils and made her feel slightly sick. Then, the odour of decomposing egg-yolk wafted disgustingly from the ends of her hair.

She opened her eyes and pulled her chair closer to the table. She had found her headline:

The Truth About Stinking Britain

Without stopping to make any more notes, Jac typed feverishly, her thoughts tumbling out and layering onto the screen in a blizzard of letters. She didn't hear a pair of high heels tip-tapping towards her, and didn't realise Miss Steele was behind her again until she spoke.

'This is promising. Very promising indeed.'

Jac's cheeks glowed, partly from the compliment, but mostly from the effort of writing. It felt as if her blood had come alive and was dancing for joy.

'Good job, Jac,' said Miss Steele.

Wow.

No adult had ever called her 'Jac' before, and it felt great.

III

Jac let herself in through the front door of the family apartment. Ignoring the note stuck to the hall mirror that said 'SHOES OFF', she walked into the kitchen and opened the fridge.

It was stacked with foil cartons in cardboard sleeves: two dozen luxury ready meals, one on top of the other, like silver ingots in a bank vault. There were bags of pre-washed salad in the cooler; fruit smoothies and champagne were chilling in the door. Jac took a lasagne and put it in the microwave, shook some salad onto a plate and made herself a drink. She wandered back into the hall to check the mail; there was a letter from her French pen friend, Colette, on the table. As she tore open the envelope she noticed that Colette had stuck sixteen stamps on it. Mad girl, thought Jac.

Colette had enclosed a couple of photos. One was a selfie of the two of them, eating triangles of peppered *socca*, sitting on the wall at Grimaud Castle in the south of France. Jac let the happy memories of that day revisit her. After taking the photo, she and Colette had run down the hill and squeezed through a hedge into the local vineyard, where they crept between the rows of vines. They dared each other to eat the unripe grapes, wincing as the sharp green juice hit the backs of their tongues. Then they made vine leaf garlands and wore them around their heads, posing like Greek goddesses.

The other picture was of Colette standing on the doorstep of her house. The evening sun was catching her nut brown hair, and a light breeze had blown a wisp of it across her cheek. She stood with her hands in the pockets of her denim pedal-pushers, a blue corduroy cap casting a slight shadow over her hazel eyes.

They had been pen friends since they were seven, and best friends since a school exchange trip a year later. Colette was kind and funny – and visiting her in France had exposed Jac to a soft, welcoming kind of family that she hadn't experienced at home. Colette could sing and dance, too, and she laughed a lot – three things Jac had never mastered.

Jac tucked the photos into the breast pocket of her school shirt and took a single piece of paper from the envelope. The letter was short, and Jac read it while the lasagne finished cooking.

Grimaud, March 23rd
My Dear Jac,

I am so sorry, my friend, but this is the last time that I can write to you.

As you know, we had to sell our computer (anyway, the internet is now shut here in France) and use the money to buy petrol and food. First my emails had to end - and now my letters, too, because the stamps are too expensive to buy.

I hope you can still write to me but you must forgive me that I cannot write back. I think that the mail trains still run once a week.

One day, I hope we can have real conversations once more.

Fondest love,
Ta amie,
Colette xx

Jac frowned. She knew that things in Europe were bad. The economy in France (and everywhere) had gone wrong. Even worse, the threat of a terrorist 'germ bomb' had forced all the European borders to close. But ... how could anybody not afford a stamp?

The microwave pinged. Jac imagined some madman in Paris setting off explosives that were full of bacteria and disease; of death and sickness spreading through France and finally reaching Grimaud. A picture of Colette getting horribly ill flashed into her mind. She pushed it out again.

She ran to her bedroom to get her MP3 player, set it to 'shuffle' and returned to the kitchen, pushing the earphones into her ears. She slid the lasagne onto a plate, took her food into the lounge and sank into the white leather sofa. She put her feet up on the coffee table and shovelled her food in with a fork, occasionally wiping her chin with her hand. When she had finished she pushed the plate across the coffee table and went to her room.

She slipped into a pair of skinny jeans and two baggy black tops, one layered over the other. She pushed a dark purple stud through the piercing on the side of her nose and pulled a charcoal grey beanie hat over her hair, grimacing at her pale skin and freckles in the mirror. She grabbed her schoolbag and started her homework.

It was nearly half past nine when she finished. She pressed her earphones back into her ears and turned the volume up to maximum. Her favourite Retro-Punk track beamed through the headphones, and she allowed her body to twist and flick to the music. She watched herself in the mirror as she danced – the lead guitarist of The Screaming Puppies pumped the E-string to fever pitch and the chorus of 'Hate You' began:

Just 'cos you're RICH
That don't give you sole rights
I'm so ANGRY it's like an itch
An' I can't sleep my rightful sleep at nights
Just 'cos I ain't working doesn't mean I can't be a
STAR
You wanna DRIVE me out
But you won't let someone like ME sit in your big,
posh car

The pulsating bass line took over her body. She wiggled her hips, eyes closed, shaking her fists above her head and stamping her heel into the floor. The second verse was even better:

I am a knife with a blade of tears
You are a bicycle …

She opened her eyes and nearly died of embarrassment. Her mum was standing in the bedroom doorway. She had a gin and tonic in one hand and a chintzy gift-bag in the other.

'Darling, what is *wrong* with using the dining room? The lounge reeks of minced beef.'

'Sorry.'

'And is it too much to spray round with the air freshener afterwards?' She kissed Jac on one cheek, but stopped short of planting another on the opposite side. 'Ugh! Tomato sauce, darling!' She tutted in disgust.

Jac smeared her cheek with her hand. Her mum held out the gift bag. 'For Colette,' she said.

'Thanks.' Jac looked inside.

'Don't thank me, darling. It was Francesca. She's a positive angel.'

Francesca was Flick Stryder's P.A. She did all the shopping for the family – except for things that got delivered.

There was a noise in the hallway and the front door banged shut.

'Your father's decided to come home, then.' Her mum downed the gin and tonic in one. 'He said he'd have dinner ready.' She turned and walked out of the door.

There was a velvet-covered box inside the gift bag: it was Colette's birthday next week. Jac opened it to find a bracelet. Hooking her fingers through a triple-loop of silver rope, she pulled it out and laid it across her wrist. At the clasp was a small heart, engraved with the words *vrais amies pour toujours* on one side and *true friends forever* on the reverse. The heart was hinged, and when it was opened up, there was a tiny pearl inside.

Francesca had also chosen some pink and black gift paper and a pretty card. Jac wrapped up the bracelet and wrote a birthday message to Colette in French.

'And don't worry – I will keep writing to you. Will sneak in some stamps next time. Have a wonderful day.

22

Take care and stay safe. Jac. X.'

She put the present in a Jiffy bag, upon which Francesca had already put the address and postage. Thoughts of a biological bomb spraying filth and death into the lungs of French children haunted Jac again – and, once more, she shut the images away in the back of her mind. On the way to the kitchen, Jac left the parcel on the hall table.

Her dad didn't look up when she walked in; he was reading some legal papers. Jac opened the fridge to see if there was any cheesecake, then hunted for the biggest spoon she could find.

'Have you done your homework properly?'

'She always does it properly, Julian.' Her mum was refilling the ice cube machine.

How would you know, thought Jac.

She drew breath and prepared to tell them about what had happened at Journalism Club. She really wanted them to know that Miss Steele was pleased with her work. But then she thought better of it. Her parents had always disapproved of her ambition to become a news reporter. They hated journalists. Except for the ones they bribed to keep on their side.

Her dad put the documents away and started pricking holes in the cellophane film of two microwave meals. Four stabs to the left; down a bit; four stabs to the right; down a bit …

'Oh for God's sake, Julian! That is so annoying!' Her mum ripped open a salad bag and the leaves flew into a bowl.

'If the holes are evenly spaced it cooks better.' (Four more stabs.)

'That's ridiculous. And do you have to use that knife?'

'The knife's fine.'

'I didn't realise you were such an expert.'

Her dad slammed the blade onto the table. 'Do you want me to cook tonight or not?' His voice was too loud now.

'Do I WANT you to cook? You never cook, of course I want you to cook!'

Jac took the cheesecake to her room. She had been invisible since her mum said the word 'annoying'. She sliced her spoon through the creamy topping into the biscuit base, and shoved a huge lump into her mouth. Her parents' voices were louder now, and her dad was threatening to leave the flat and eat dinner at his club. Jac chewed slowly. The cheesecake tasted of nothing, and her stomach no longer wanted it.

The front door slammed for the second time that evening and her mum swore loudly down the hallway. There were footsteps, an angry rattle of the drinks cabinet in the living room, and another bang as her mum shut herself inside her office and began a heated business call.

Jac put her plate on the floor and curled up on her bed. She pulled her jumper upwards so it was half over her face, then withdrew her hands into her sleeves, clasping the cuffs from the inside.

The Screaming Puppies soundtrack raged into her ears through the headphones and the pumping bass became her heartbeat.

Not for the first time, she fell asleep on top of the bedclothes with her clothes on.

IV

The school floors had been polished over the weekend and the corridors smelled of a mixture of beeswax and turpentine.

As Jac approached her form room, the door flew open and Fabian and Rufus fell out, hands grasped around each other's throats. Half the class tumbled out behind them, camera phones held high, stamping their feet and shouting 'Fight! Fight! Fight!' Rufus pushed Fabian against the door opposite and Fabian squashed a hand into Rufus's face. Rufus gained the advantage and dragged Fabian to the ground; Fabian stole a swift punch to Rufus's stomach and the pair rolled over and over.

Year Ten students appeared from other doorways and swarmed into the corridor. Jac shoved her way to the front in time to see Rufus plant a heavy punch to the side of Fabian's head. Fabian let out a groan; his body went limp and his eyes flickered shut. Rufus sat back on his heels and saluted in victory.

'You pig!' Jac rushed forward and thumped Rufus with her bag, but before she could reach Fabian to comfort him, he sprang upright and hit Rufus so hard on the nose that it began to bleed. Completely taken aback, Rufus started to cry.

25

Fabian stood up and bowed theatrically to everyone. 'Once again, Rufus has failed to appreciate my acting skills,' he said. 'See me 'play dead' again soon in 'Julius Caesar'. Ladies and gentlemen, thank you very much.'

A couple of people cheered. Rufus looked at Fabian in astonishment, someone gave him a tissue to mop up the blood, and a posse of teachers arrived and ordered everyone back to their rooms. Mr Figgis announced that every class on the lower corridor would be given a week's detention.

'And you three – headmaster's office. Now.'

Ten minutes later, Jac and Fabian were waiting on the bench outside Mr Sterne's room, sitting shoulder to shoulder.

'What were you scrapping about?'

'It doesn't matter.' Fabian's cheeks coloured.

'I didn't know you could fight!'

'Neither did I.'

Jac laughed through her nose. She gave Fabian a nudge and he nudged her back.

'I'll tell Sterne you had nothing to do with it,' he said.

Rufus arrived from the medical room and sat at the other end of the bench. His nose was red and swollen.

'Watcha, Rudolph,' said Jac.

Rufus snorted. 'Has either of you two actually got any friends, apart from each other?' he said.

Jac had no comeback. For her, at least, the answer was 'no'. Except for Colette.

'Actually, Fabie-Baby does have a friend. A little special friend. Bet you haven't told Jac about him, have you?'

Jac turned to look at Fabian, but he wouldn't look

26

back at her.

Mr Sterne came out of his office and asked all three of them to come in. To Jac's surprise, Rufus didn't mention that she'd hit him with her bag. As she got up to leave, Fabian whispered that Rufus didn't want anyone knowing he'd been thumped by a girl. Rufus glared. Jac wiped a bogey on Rufus's back whilst thanking Mr Sterne for his understanding, and then she left.

She was on her way to the girls' toilets when she bumped into Miss Steele.

'I hear you were involved in an incident this morning. Sounds rather dramatic.'

Jac fiddled with the zip on her bag. 'I was only trying to help. I thought Fabian had got knocked out. I've never hit anyone before.'

Miss Steele smiled. 'I'm glad to hear it,' she said. 'But you weren't afraid to stick up for your friend. In journalism, if you want to get yourself a good story, you gotta be feisty.'

She looked up and down the empty corridor.

'I'm glad I bumped into you. I want to talk to you about something.' She pulled a leaflet out of her pocket. 'It's a college for young journalists. Just a few miles out of London.'

Jac took the leaflet and looked at a photograph of a tall, sleek glass building.

'The Institute is looking for high-achieving, apprentice reporters,' said Miss Steele. 'Original thinkers who will fight for a cause.' She tapped the paper with an immaculately manicured fingernail. 'Little Miss Average need *not* apply. I think you should be there, Jac.'

A rush of excitement spread upwards from somewhere in Jac's gut, up through her chest and into her face. She knew she was blushing.

'It's a six month residential course. You do regular schoolwork there, too, so St Philomena's will release you. Do you think your parents would let you go?'

Jac didn't care what they thought.

'They have a unique application process,' Miss Steele explained, pointing to a series of bullet points printed inside. 'There are five projects to complete.' She pursed her lips. 'But the projects are tough. Designed to test you. There are strict deadlines, too. You write a report at the end of each assignment and you submit the five completed articles in a portfolio. Then you are considered for the course.'

She took a pen from her handbag and scribbled a date on the top corner of the leaflet.

'They are holding introductory interviews in the first week of the Easter vacation. One day only.' She unclicked her pen and returned it to her bag. 'You miss it, you miss out for another six months.'

The clasp on the bag snapped shut.

'The course starts in September. Top three students get their portfolio published in a major newspaper. Phone the number on the back; tell them I recommended you.' She smiled. 'Now – you'll be late for class.'

Jac found it hard to say thank you without sounding gushy like her mother. Her cheeks burned a hot red for the second time.

Miss Steele strode away. Jac read the phone number on the back of the leaflet, her thumb already dialling it on an imaginary keypad. She flipped the leaflet over. The design was bold. Glossy black writing on a pearl white background. Even the choice of font excited her:

JASMINE
Journalism and Social Media: Institute of Excellence

you are our future

As Miss Steele's perfume faded, the smell of beeswax and turpentine drifted up from the floor. But Jac had no sensation of the corridor beneath her feet.

She was walking on air.

V

When Jac got home her parents were already in. She could tell by the way they were laughing that they were halfway through their second bottle of pink champagne. She walked into the lounge to find her mum sitting on her dad's lap, fondling his hair. He slapped her playfully on the leg and she squealed.

'Hi,' said Jac, trying not to look at them. There was only one reason they were behaving like this: they had won a case.

'Darling!' Her mum slid sideways onto the sofa and waved tipsily. 'Get yourself a glass and celebrate with us.'

Jac picked up the bottle of Bollinger and poured a couple of centimetres of pink froth into a glass. Her dad stood up.

'To victory,' he said.

They raised their glasses.

'To the Better Bedcovers Movement,' said her mum.

'Those idiots at SUPPORT should have got themselves a better lawyer,' said her dad.

'Three thousand pounds each in damages for the victims!' Her mum hiccupped. 'And a big fat commission for us, darling!'

Jac decided to take advantage of her parents' good mood and tell them about her conversation with Miss Steele. Maybe she could get them so drunk they would agree to let her go on the journalism course. She poured them both a large top-up.

'And there's more good news, darling! We've decided to spend our commission on a little holiday. To Saint Tropez.'

'To France?' said Jac. 'How?' The thought of getting sick from some invisible disease, thanks to a bomb that showered germs everywhere, really scared her. She didn't want to go.

'We've booked a private jet, darling. There's a little airfield in Kent we can use.'

'But what about the border closure? And the terrorists?'

'It's not as bad as everyone makes out,' said her dad.

'It turns out the whole bomb thing really isn't true, darling,' said her mum. 'Our friend in the government said so. Lots of VIP people are having little holidays. It's fine!'

'But they said on the news ...' said Jac.

'Oh for God's sake, Jacqueline!' Her dad's face darkened. 'There's no threat – they just haven't told anyone yet.' His eyes flashed angrily. 'So we're going. And don't you go round telling your schoolmates what we've told you. Otherwise everyone will want to go abroad and it'll be hard to get a seat on the jet. If they ask, we're flying down to the house in Dorset. Understood?'

Jac shrugged.

'And don't look like that. You'll be near enough to visit that pen friend of yours.'

It was worth putting her fears aside to see Colette,

thought Jac.   Maybe she could spend all of the
holiday with Colette's family.

'OK ... when?'

'First week of the Easter holidays.'

A pang of horror stabbed Jac in the chest.   That
was the same week as the JASMINE interviews.

'No! I can't come! I've got something I need to
do.'

'Don't be silly, darling. What could you possibly
have to do?'

Her dad glared. 'If I've gone to the expense of
booking a private jet for a family holiday you WILL
be there.'

There was no point in arguing – she'd learnt that
a long time ago. Her head dropped, and she turned
and walked away. 'I've got homework to do. I'll get
my dinner later.'

Another champagne cork popped as she closed
the door. They had already forgotten about her.

She ran into her room and dived onto the bed.
Maybe it was the alcohol in her blood but she felt a
rage she had never felt before.

She punched her pillow hard. A blow by the left
fist was followed by another from the right, over and
over, anger spraying out in invisible sparks with
every strike. Furious words spat out with the same
rhythm as her punches:

THIS - IS - THE - FIRST - TIME - I'VE - EVER -
FELT - REALLY - REALLY - HAPPY - AND - THEY -
JUST - HAVE - TO - RUIN - IT.

Tears fired from her eyes. Her arms started to
burn from overwork and the punching slowed until
she had just enough strength to thump out six final
beats:

WHAT --- AM --- I --- GOING --- TO --- DO?

VI

'Are you kidding?' Miss Steele's pristinely pinked lips curled disdainfully. 'Didn't you tell your parents you've got something more important to do?'

'I'm sorry,' said Jac.

'Is that it?' Miss Steele put her hands on her hips. 'How hard did you try to get out of it?'

Jac didn't know how to answer. She was sworn to secrecy over the France trip. 'It's difficult ...'

'Journalism is difficult, Jac. You gotta take every opportunity that comes your way.'

Why didn't Miss Steele understand that when a fourteen-year-old goes to war with her parents, the parents always win? Jac felt tears brewing in the corners of her eyes and looked away.

Miss Steele's voice cooled. 'Look. Maybe it's for the best. Maybe you should give up now. Perhaps you haven't got what it takes.'

'I *have* got what it takes!'

Miss Steele didn't answer and turned her attention to a bit of dirt on the toe of her shoe. 'Maybe you should stick to less ambitious projects.'

Burning with shame, Jac turned her back on Miss Steele before the teardrops got any bigger. She bit the inside of her mouth and left the room.

VII

The engines of the private jet hummed monotonously. Jac swallowed a smoked salmon canapé without chewing and frowned at the clouds drifting below.

Her mum was drinking champagne again, loudly chatting up the young, male flight attendant. Jac pushed her earphones into her ears to block out the embarrassing comments and the even more embarrassing laugh. Across the aisle, her dad sipped a cup of Columbian coffee and glared into his newspaper.

The flight seemed to be lasting forever. With no-one to talk to she was forced to listen to her own thoughts, and she didn't like what she was thinking. She squirmed in the luxury leather seat: Miss Steele's unkind words were still haunting her.

The plane tilted, sending Jac's glass sliding across her lap tray. Down below, the patchwork fields of France moved slowly by. Her dad finished reading the paper and angrily folded it into quarters; her mum simpered flirtatiously at the flight attendant as he collected the coffee cups.

Her smartphone vibrated in her pocket. It was a text from Fabian.

Have you cheered up yet? :)

As she typed in her reply, the pilot announced that the plane was beginning its descent towards the airport, and she fastened her seatbelt.

NO

The jet engines howled into overdrive. She switched off her phone, and stared crossly of out the window, watching the land rise up towards her.

VIII

A woman in a pale pink mini skirt and jacket escorted them out of the airport and into a limousine. The door closed with a swish and the limo pulled away.

As it gathered speed, Jac could hear somebody driving alongside them. It sounded like a motorbike. She tried to peer through the tinted windows but could see nothing. The limo was travelling very fast, and she gripped the seat every time they took a bend in the road. When they finally stopped in the villa complex, Jac heard a set of wheels screech and accelerate away. She jumped out of the car and peered through the hotel gates: a plume of dust was disappearing into the distance. A ripple of heat haze rose on the horizon and magnified the bike – and, for a split second, Jac was convinced the biker had a rocket launcher on their back.

The entrance hall of the holiday complex was beautiful, with water cascading from a glass fountain. A bellboy in a braided uniform showed them to their villa: three bedrooms plus two enormous, marble bathrooms, two reception rooms and a patio overlooking the gardens.

'I'm hungry,' said Jac.

'Phone room service, darling. Dinner's not until eight.' Her mum put her laptop on the couch and found some gin in the mini-bar. Her dad set up his computer on a table in the corner. Within seconds, he was immersed in his work.

Her mum planted a boozy kiss on Jac's cheek. She lifted her glass, and the ice clinked against the sides.

'Happy holidays, darling!' After a moment, she, too, was engrossed in the files on her computer.

Jac ordered herself a sandwich, then sat on the patio and switched her phone on. Fabian had been texting her:

Have you cheered up? x

Have you cheered up NOW you grumpy cow :)

You've switched your phone off haven't you YOU STUFFED CLOAKBAG OF GUTS (Shakespeare, in case ur wondering)

More Shakespeare THERE'S A DIVINITY THAT SHAPES OUR ENDS

I know things will work out for you with JASMINE x0x stress ye not!

Jac smiled and breathed in the warm, seaside air.

Thanx best friend xx
Less than an hour off the plane my parents are working and I don't exist

Room service arrived with her sandwich, and Fabian replied:

My dad hasn't come home from the office for three nights usual boring top secret crisis Mum treating me like a three year old I ... am ... slowly suffocating ... her ... love ... is ... the ... devil's ...poison ...

you drama queen ur right though mums are seriously toxic

WOMAN THOU ART A NEEDSOME BEAST

Shakespeare?

No I just made it up

Ha ha

Have to go ...
DON'T LOSE SIGHT OF YOUR DREAMS AND THEY'LL COME TRUE XXX
BE THE BRAVE GIRL I KNOW AND LOVE

Thanx again
LYT x

Fabian was such a tonic. Be brave, he said – and his words made her feel herself again.

The sea breeze caressed her skin and pulled gently at the fabric of her top, as if it were calling her to adventure. She went to her room, threw a few things into a beach bag and rearranged her hair in front of the mirror. She could get a cab to Colette's and be back easily in time for dinner. It would be fun to surprise her – and hopefully she would end up staying with Colette's family the most of the week.

'I'm going for a walk,' she told her parents.

'Mm-mm,' said her mum.

Downstairs in the lobby, Jac asked the receptionist where she could get a taxi. The receptionist looked alarmed.

'*Non, Mademoiselle!* You cannot leave the villa compound! It is not safe!'

'Oh, I thought the germ-bomb thing wasn't really true,' said Jac.

'*Pardon? Non!*' The receptionist waved her hand in dismay. 'You must only walk in the gardens,' she said.

Jac shrugged. She walked across the entrance hall and through an archway at the back. The grounds of the compound were beautiful. But the tall, whitewashed walls made her feel trapped, and she longed to be the other side of them.

As she wandered through an orange grove she heard the clatter of saucepans through a window and caught the smell of frying onions. She strolled over to have a look. Her heart quickened: there was bound to be a back exit out of the kitchen! A white chef's coat hung on a peg on an open door; she took it, slipped it on and walked inside.

The kitchen was hot. The head chef was shouting and everyone was stressed. Nobody noticed her – until someone handed her a bowl of beetroot, shouting '*Coupez-les en julienne!*'

'*Oui, Monsieur Chef,*' she replied.

She took the bowl to a workstation in the far corner. She gave the beetroot to a sou chef who was barely older than her.

'*Coupez-les en julienne!*' she shouted, and the young cook nervously began slicing. Jac backed away and slipped through the nearby fire door.

There was a row of dustbins in the yard and, beyond that, a padlocked gate. As Jac reached it, a motorbike approached, so she ducked behind one of the bins. The bike crawled past, the rider's head scanning from side to side. As the sound of the engine died away, Jac went to the gate and watched. Black bike, black leather – and a big, black gun. The rider spoke into a walkie-talkie and his boots gleamed in the sunshine.

When he had gone, Jac climbed over the gate and jumped onto the pavement the other side. She took off the white coat and hung it on the gatepost.

'Colette, here I come,' she breathed, and set off down the dusty track to the outskirts of Saint Tropez.

IX

The houses on the edge of town didn't look right.

The shadows on the whitewashed walls should have moved with Jac, but they didn't. As she got closer she realised that the whole street was a painted façade, like a film set. Strange. She kept walking until she found a place where the wooden screens had warped in the sun, and there was a gap big enough to squeeze through. Behind her, she heard the purr of a motorbike as the armed rider made another circuit of the villa complex. She breathed in and pushed herself between the panels of wood.

The suburbs of Saint Tropez lay before her. Barren, fire-damaged, deserted. No people, no cars. No noise except for the distant cry of a flock of gulls. The coffee-coloured bricks and cinnamon roof tiles, once home to the rich, the successful and the fabulous, were now shabby shells filled with rubble and broken glass. As she looked around in disbelief, an emaciated rat scuttled under a burnt-out car.

She sat on a low wall and drank slowly from her water bottle. She felt sick – what had happened here? It was like something out of a disaster movie. A rumbling noise came from behind her and she leapt up. A chimney pot tumbled into the street, in a shower of brick and dust. Every nerve cell in her body told her to run back to the safety of the villa. But her head said 'no'. She should stay calm and try to find out what was going on.

She looked at the map she'd brought with her, but it was impossible to follow because the street signs were missing. She decided to set off on foot in the general direction of Grimaud – Colette would know why Saint Tropez was like this. Maybe, if she kept walking, she would meet someone who could show her where to get a bus.

The sun warmed her skin and a trickle of sweat ran down her back. The only sound was the zip jangling on her bag as she walked. She passed through the remains of a small square and stopped again for a drink.

There was a noise on the other side of the street and she turned around. For a moment she thought she saw a girl crawling through a hole in a wall. She called out, but no-one answered. Then a seagull was startled by something and flapped, mewling, into the sky.

There were child-like footsteps behind her, and somebody hit her over the back of the head. She swooned and dropped to the ground. Forcing her eyes open, she saw several pairs of small feet swarming round her. Nobody spoke. Somebody kicked her in the back; someone else pulled her by the ears and another held her tight.

They grabbed her bag, and now they were after her money belt. She tried to wriggle out of the way and kick them but they were too many. Bony little hands dug into her trouser pockets and took whatever they could find. Her watch was snatched from her wrist and she squealed in pain as her necklace was ripped off with such force that the friction burned her skin. They prised the rings from her clenched fingers, pinching the back of her hand until she yielded. Then a skinny finger poked its way into her left nostril and dug around until it had removed her nose stud. But they didn't stop there.

Somebody undid her shoes and took them. The rest of them pulled off her top and held her down while they stole her jeans. She let out a low moan when she realised what was going to happen next. They rolled her over onto her side, and two sets of grubby fingers wormed their way under her bra strap.

There was a shout, and the crackling of machine gun bullets rang down the street. In a flash, her assailants scattered and disappeared. Jac protected her head with her hands and cringed, desperate to sink away, safe, into the earth. There were heavy footsteps and pair of knee-length leather boots stood beside her.

'*Vous allez bien?*' said a man's voice. He bent down to touch her.

'Get your filthy hands off me!' yelled Jac.

The man stepped back. '*N'ayez pas peur,*' he said. 'There is nothing to be afraid of.'

He took off his jacket and threw it gently towards her.

'Please,' he said. 'Put it on.'

Jac sat up and draped the jacket over her shoulders, pulling it close around her midriff. She turned herself sideways, too shy to face the man head-on, and sneaked a glance at him. He was in his twenties, over six feet tall, with tousled brown hair. With his jacket removed, she could see that, as well as his machine gun, he was carrying a belt of hand grenades and a pistol.

'*Je m'appelle Jean-Luc,*' he said.

'Jac. Jacqueline.'

'*Bonjour, Jac.*' He put out his hand to help her up.

'*Merci,*' she said. She still couldn't look him in the eye, but she was glad that he was there.

Jean-Luc took her to what had once been a bistro, although there was nothing left inside it.

'All the tables and chairs – taken and burnt,' he said. 'People need a fire more than they need somewhere to sit.'

He used a flint lighter to spark up some dried grass inside an old biscuit tin. 'The tablecloths were taken to make clothes.' He smiled wryly. 'For a time, everyone in this neighbourhood wore red-check. A few blocks away, at *Maison Pierre,* the tables were covered in green and white. You could tell where people lived by the tablecloths they were wearing.'

He put a billycan into the midst of the flames inside the tin. As he continued to speak, he added handfuls of grass, occasionally pausing to blow gently on the fire.

'All the *aménagements intérieurs* … all the ovens, lights, water pipes … all were taken and sold in exchange for food. Even the electric wires - ripped out and stripped. The plastic on the outside is valuable, too. I sleep on a cushion which is full of tiny pieces of this plastic. It is not comfortable, but it is better than the floor.'

It wasn't long before the water inside the billycan had heated up. Jean-Luc tipped some granules into a white plastic cup; the sort that is normally thrown away after a single use. This one was so stained it was more brown than white.

'May I ask you, please, not to split my precious cup? It is the only one I've got.'

He poured on the hot water and held it out to Jac.

'Dandelion root coffee. It is not so bad.'

Jac sipped it slowly. 'It's piggin' awful,' she said.

Jean-Luc raised an eyebrow and reached out to take it off her.

'I didn't say I wouldn't drink it,' said Jac.

'You are a cheeky girl!' he said. 'But save a little for me, if you please.'

The twinkle vanished from his eyes and his brow furrowed. 'And now you must tell me what you are doing here.'

'Are you kidding?' said Jac. She slurped a mouthful of coffee and handed back the cup. 'You're going to tell *me* what the heck is going on in this place!'

Jean-Luc's frown deepened, then his forehead relaxed again. He nodded.

'Of course. You are British. Your Internet is being manipulated. You do not know what has happened to your European friends. You believe that there is a terrorist threat. A biological bomb. But this is a lie, designed to keep you away and stop you from seeing the truth.'

Jac sensed a big story, and she felt a thrill down her spine. But a shadow clouded Jean-Luc's eyes as he gathered his thoughts, and the excited frisson Jac had felt at first turned cold and scuttled up the back of her neck. She hugged her knees and waited for him to reveal Saint Tropez's dark secret.

X

'Europe is broken. Broke. Bust.'

Jean-Luc took a deep mouthful of coffee and swallowed hard.

'Nobody here has any money. The banks went bad, the money grew more and more worthless – and now it's worth nothing at all.'

Jac looked uncomfortably at the hard, dirty floor. 'You mean it's not just Saint Tropez that's wrecked like this?' She was thinking about Colette. 'What about Grimaud?'

'It is the whole of France.' His forehead folded into a series of small ridges. 'In fact it is worse than that. It is the whole of Europe.'

Jean-Luc ran his fingers through his hair, and his blue eyes watched Jac as she chewed hard on her thumbnail.

'Yes – it is a lot to take in,' he said. 'Now perhaps you understand why everything is gone – and why the young children were not afraid to take your things.'

She understood. When people have nothing, they will do anything to keep themselves alive.

Jean-Luc offered her another sip of his coffee and she took it gladly.

'But what about my holiday villa?' she asked. 'It's totally blinging.'

'There are still a few people who have money. And they want to make more money. So they trade with America, Asia and Great Britain. And everybody pretends there is nothing wrong.'

Jac got up and paced around the room. She was really worried about Colette now. 'I'm sorry,' she said, 'but I need to find my friend.'

'Ah, Grimaud,' said Jean-Luc, nodding. 'I wondered why this small French town was of interest to you ...' He stroked the stubble on his chin. '*Non.* It is too dangerous.'

'I'll go on my own, then,' said Jac.

'Absolutely not.'

'Absolutely *yes!*' Jac got up and moved towards the door.

'Those children were easy to scare away,' said Jean-Luc. 'But there are people out there who are more difficult to deal with.'

'I've nothing left for them to steal,' said Jac. 'Unless you're worried about your crappy jacket.'

Jean-Luc looked furious. He picked Jac up by the elbows and carried her to the opposite side of the room, away from the door.

'Put me down, you big bully ...'

'Shut up! You stupid little girl!'

Jac was so shocked her mouth fell open.

'You are so naïve!' he said. 'Believe, me, there are things these people can take from you that you will *never* be able to get back. Things that no young girl should have to lose.'

He made an exasperated noise and let her go. 'But I see you are still determined to see your friend.'

He turned away for a few moments, rubbing his

chin. When he faced her again, the anger had gone. For a split second, his eyes burned and flickered with ideas ... then he smiled and murmured to himself.

'Very well,' he said. 'You must come with me.'

There was a dilapidated outhouse at the back of the bistro. Inside, hidden under a rotten tarpaulin was an ancient motorbike. Jean-Luc wheeled it into the yard and climbed astride it.

'I thought you said everything metal had been stolen,' said Jac.

Jean-Luc patted the weapon strapped to his torso. 'When you have a gun, you have a few privileges,' he said. 'Get on. And hold tight.'

Jac threaded her arms around Jean-Luc's waist. As he revved up the engine, she curled her bare feet round the cold metal foot rests and buried her face in Jean-Luc's shirt. The bike wobbled and she gasped, convinced that she would fall to the ground. She was about to scream at Jean-Luc to forget the whole idea when they surged forward, accelerating down the narrow passage at the side of the bistro and out onto the street.

Within minutes they were speeding through the suburbs of Saint Tropez. Abandoned luxury villas stood on both sides of the street. A pack of youths howled from a rooftop and threw stones as they passed; Jean-Luc skilfully avoided the missiles with a series of twists and turns. Soon the wrecked buildings gave way to fields and orchards, and the road opened out into a broad highway. Jean-Luc slowed the bike and gestured towards a community of ramshackle houses built from junk.

'In the countryside, people are more civilised,' he shouted. 'They can grow food, so they are happy to share with each other. It is safer out here.'

He waved to a woman sitting on top of a rusty van with no wheels. At first, Jac thought she was guarding a giant telescope, but she was actually looking down the sights of some sort of missile-launcher. The woman waved cheerily back.

'As you can see, they know me,' he shouted. 'She will not shoot.'

'Glad to hear it,' shouted Jac.

They swept along the highway for a few miles, then Jean-Luc stopped at a small settlement and traded a jerry can of petrol for some apples, bread, potatoes and two dead rabbits. They set off again, and it wasn't long before the town of Grimaud was in sight.

Soon afterwards, Jean-Luc parked in a lay-by and paid a group of teenagers a loaf of bread to guard the bike until they returned.

'Now,' he said. 'The address?'

'Rue Lafayette,' said Jac. 'I think it's this way.'

The narrow, rambling streets of Grimaud were silent. The higgledy-piggledy houses looked bleak as Jac and Jean-Luc wound their way uphill towards the neighbourhood where Colette lived.

A hollow-eyed girl stared at them through a glassless window and a skinny dog with nasty yellow teeth growled at them from behind a garden wall. The last time Jac had visited Grimaud there had been children laughing and running in the street, grandfathers playing cards in the dappled shade of the olive trees and the occasional scooter purring lazily past in the cool of the day.

'This is awful,' she said to Jean-Luc. 'How did it start?'

'Greedy people. Governments got into debt and they needed to save money. They tried to make cuts

– but everybody complained. So the governments gave in and spent more money instead.'

Sounds like Britain, thought Jac.

'The debt spiralled out of control and one by one, the countries of Europe crashed like dominoes.'

Jean-Luc's eyes were aflame. 'You must listen to me, Jac. Everyone is saying that Great Britain is the next domino to fall.'

But Jac was only half paying attention: they had arrived at Rue Lafayette.

As she hurried towards Colette's house she realised that her legs were shaking. For the first time since the Saint Tropez children had stolen her shoes, she became aware of the harshness of the road under her bare feet and the grit between her toes.

'Colette?' she called, but there was no answer.

Jean-Luc climbed the step to the front door, knocked loudly and shouted, *'Bonjour! Y a-t-il quelqu'un à la maison?'*

He knocked again, hard, and the door swung open with a creak.

'Wait here,' he said.

He disappeared inside for ages. Jac could hear him moving around, occasionally calling out as he made his way from room to room. Eventually he returned. There was fire in his eyes again.

'There is nobody here. From the look of the place I think it has been empty for some time.'

Jac felt faint. She reached for Jean-Luc's arm and he steadied her.

'I think you must return to your villa,' he murmured. He picked her up and carried her downhill to the bike.

They rode back in silence, Jac pressed against Jean-Luc's back like a baby koala clinging to its mother. Finally the bike screeched to a halt at the back of the villa complex.

'I promise you I will find out what happened to your friend,' said Jean-Luc. 'I will return here as soon as I can. In the meantime, you must stay indoors. I cannot always be here to protect you.'

'OK,' said Jac.

Using the bike as a step-up, Jean-Luc helped her climb over the wall into the orange grove. She heard the bike roar away. The receptionist saw her as she entered the foyer, looked at her half-clad, dirty body with horror and called the security guard.

'Excuse me!' The receptionist called sharply in French.

'Excuse *you*,' called Jac.

The security guard appeared and lunged towards her. His hands slipped on the fabric of Jean-Luc's jacket and Jac ran away, leaving the guard behind her.

The villa door was unlocked. Jac brushed off as much dirt as she could from her legs and feet and stuck her head into the room. Her parents were sitting exactly where she had left them.

'Dinner in five minutes, darling,' said her mum. She didn't look up. 'And make sure you wear something nice.'

Jac walked into her bedroom, removed the only three items of clothing she had on, and jumped in the shower.

XI

Jac watched her ice cream sundae slowly melt into a pool of creamy soup. Since she had said goodbye to Jean-Luc five days ago the hours had been crawling by. She felt lost without her phone, without Fabian's texts – and without Colette.

She had spent as much time as she could in the orange grove, listening out for Jean-Luc's bike. But, after a while, she would get sick of the heavy, citrussy scent leaking from the fruit and return to the hotel room, only to be driven mad by her parents tapping on their laptops. So she would retreat to the patio with a snack, which she rarely ate, until the itch to wait for the bike returned. Then she would go back to her deckchair in the shade of the orange trees and listen out all over again.

In the warmth of the patio sun, she fished out a frosted grape with her spoon, contemplated eating it, then dropped it back into the melted ice cream with a splash. Then her mum appeared, trying to hurry in a pair of strapless mules.

'Darling! Good news!' She stopped, and regarded Jac's ice cream. 'Or bad news. Depending on how you look at it.'

'What?'

'Daddy's been offered a big, big, case. Huge, darling.'

'Sounds … great.' Jac pushed a cherry round the inside of the bowl.

'It's high profile but terribly hush-hush.' Her mum lowered her voice. 'Some silly politician's got himself into of a bit of a pickle. It means we have to go home straight away. Our plane leaves in two hours and there's a limo waiting outside.'

'No way!' Jac thumped the table in frustration. They couldn't possibly leave before she had found out about Colette.

'Oh don't be silly, darling – we can have another holiday in July.' Her mum looked at the sundae dish. 'And Daddy can buy you a new ice cream at the airport if you like.'

Why did they still treat her like a toddler? 'Don't be piggin' ridiculous!' Jac shouted. 'I don't care about the stupid ice …'

Her mum interrupted. 'Saving the reputation of a top politician is *not* ridiculous. Really, Jac, you are so spoilt.'

It was no use saying anything else. They went inside to pack; Jac tried to delay leaving for as long as she could and another argument flared up when her dad told her she was being childish.

After locking herself in the bathroom for as long as she dared, then running back to the orange grove because she said she had lost her sunglasses, they were finally in the foyer.

As her dad, red-faced and furious, settled the bill, Jac heard the sound of a motorbike engine in the hotel forecourt. She rushed outside, forcing the bike to skid to a halt in front of her. The driver lifted the visor of his helmet and swore at her in French. Of course it wasn't Jean-Luc! It was the outrider paid to escort their limousine to the airport. He grunted, checked his weapon and waited for the car to leave.

The driver asked Jac for her bags, but she told him she wanted to wait until her parents came. She hoped it might delay their departure by a few more seconds, but it was never going to be enough.

A shower of gravel flew through the air from somewhere, the pieces bouncing around her on the driveway. She turned around and her heart jumped: Jean-Luc was hiding in the archway that led to the orange grove. He gestured to her to come over, staying out of sight of the guards and security cameras. Ignoring her parents' anger, Jac ran to meet him.

Jean-Luc embraced her, and she knew from his dark expression that something was wrong.

'My dear Jac,' he said. He looked over to the limo and at Jac's parents calling and waving from inside. 'And I see I have to be quick.'

'Is Colette OK?' she said.

'It seems that a gang from Toulon came to Grimaud in search of plunder about five weeks ago. In Rue Lafayette they found your friend. Unfortunately she was wearing an expensive silver bracelet which they tried to remove from her. In the struggle that followed ...' Jean-Luc fought with himself to continue. 'In the ensuing struggle ... I regret – your friend Colette was murdered.'

A sickening numbness coursed through Jac's body. Jean-Luc's words sounded hollow and meaningless. Yet, simultaneously, she felt a pain that she had never felt before.

'I am so sorry, Jac.' His eyes were wild, animated. 'I know there is nothing more I can say.'

She looked around desperately. Her dad had leaned into the front of the car and was honking the car horn repeatedly. In a daze, she turned away from Jean-Luc and started to walk off.

Jean-Luc caught hold of her arm. 'Please. Remember what I told you. Britain has become too greedy. She will destroy herself, like all the other countries. She *will* be the next to fall. Promise me you will not leave here and do nothing. I cannot bear to think of you having to live and die like your friend Colette.'

Jac nodded and the world seemed to spin around her.

The limousine skidded towards her on the gravel and a rear door opened. Jean-Luc slipped away as she climbed inside. Her parents were shouting now, but it sounded like nothing more than a vague, unpleasant noise – like bad music on the car stereo.

The tinted windows closed and the car wheels spun and squealed in a cloud of dust. The air conditioning came on and created a deathly chill in the back of the car, and they sped out of the villa complex and hurtled towards the airport, the armed outrider tearing behind them.

XII

Crisply dressed cabin crew served champagne cocktails garnished with twists of orange and strawberries. Well-fed holidaymakers spouted meaningless small talk to her parents in between mouthfuls of premium caviar.

Jac gripped her sick bag so hard that it disintegrated between her sweaty fingers. She had already vomited twice: once in the limo and again at the airport. Now there was nothing left to throw up. Every time she thought of Colette – every time she remembered the silver bracelet which she had given her – her stomach convulsed and she retched again. And then she tried to bury the thoughts somewhere where they couldn't hurt her.

Yet the shock made her burn with a determination she had never felt before. Something good *had* to come out of this. Otherwise she may as well rush to the nearest emergency exit, fling open the door and throw herself out of the plane. She wanted to stand up and scream the truth to everyone: that, far below this luxury bubble in the sky, her best friend had died, and Europe was dying.

But adults didn't listen to children. She'd tried to talk to her parents about it in the departure lounge, but her mum had said she was being silly and her dad told her not to have 'dangerous opinions'. He had shouted at her, saying that repeating those ideas could get Jac 'into a lot of trouble'. So she kept quiet, feeling like a bomb that was going to explode. As soon has the plane had flown into British airspace, she had borrowed her mum's smartphone and searched the internet for information about Europe – but Jean-Luc had been right: it was as if the poverty and devastation didn't exist. Somebody had gone to a lot of trouble to tell a massive, massive lie. Stuck in her seat and smouldering with impatience, she knew she had to do something – but what was there to do?

Everything she had learned in France circulated through her mind ... spiralling, wheeling and revolving like a weird hallucination. Time was crawling by ... or was it? She looked out of the window and saw that they were over Kent already.

The next thing she knew the plane had landed.

An hour or so afterwards, a taxi dropped her parents off at their office, leaving Jac and the luggage to travel home alone.

Feelings of rage and grief still bubbled within her, but the rattle of the London traffic cleared her head, and she began to formulate a plan.

By the time she arrived at the apartment, she knew exactly what she was going to do. She had a story to tell – an explosive, urgent story that couldn't wait. A story that *might* be listened to if it had the right exposure at the right time. Nobody cared about the rantings of a stroppy schoolgirl – but *everybody* would pay attention if a top student at a prestigious journalism college got her story published in a major newspaper ...

Her mum had given her a spare phone, and a

57

credit card to pay the cab driver and, as soon as she got indoors, she booked another taxi. She showered, dressed warmly and packed a change of clothes. Soon, a black cab appeared in the street. Jac waved from the window and let herself out of the front door.

'Where to, love?'

She climbed onto the back seat and spoke to the driver through the intercom. His head was shaved, and Jac could see every single hair follicle as it waited to sprout. She saw individual specks of dust on the windows and flecks of fibre on the seat and walls. She had never seen the world as clearly as she saw it now.

'The JASMINE Institute, please,' she said. 'And I want you to take me there as quickly as you can.'

XIII

It was nearly midnight when the taxi arrived at JASMINE.

'It don't look like there's anybody there, love,' said the cabbie.

Jac stared up at the dimly lit giant, glass cuboid. 'I'm not going in – I'm meeting a friend.'

'Do you want me to wait?'

'It's fine. They'll be here in two minutes.'

As the cab drove away, Jac walked up to the main entrance and peered in. A sleek reception area with funky furniture was silhouetted against the low energy security lights. Beyond, a corridor stretched backwards to what looked like infinity and a shiny, cylindrical lift stood dormant on the ground floor.

Jac knew from the brochure that the Institute was surrounded by gardens. She left the drop-off bay and walked round the side of the building, out of the glare of the street lamps. Soft earth squished beneath her feet as she accidentally trod through a flowerbed.

'Ow! That hurt – you piggin' prickle!'

She pressed her lips to the place where she felt the scratch, and tasted blood. Another rose bush snagged her jumper and she swore. As she walked off the bed she fell over and landed face first on the lawn. The grass felt damp and smelled fresh. She rolled over onto her back and looked around.

There was a large, shadowy shape to her right: probably some sort of shrub. She pulled herself up and crawled underneath it. She opened her rucksack, took out an unbuttered baguette that she'd found at the back of a cupboard at home, and chewed slowly.

She checked the time: 12.23 a.m. She pulled her beanie over her ears and eyes and used the rucksack as a pillow. God, it felt uncomfortable. But it was good to be on her own in the middle of nowhere, with nobody to tell her what to do. An unpleasant, murky smell like dirty feathers seemed to be coming from nearby. A stone dug into her shoulder, but before she could find the energy to move and get rid of it, she had fallen asleep. She woke again at dawn and tossed and turned in a bored stupor for hours.

The sound of a delivery lorry reversing into a driveway at the side of the building roused her. Maybe she had got back to sleep after all. She sat up: it was 9:30 a.m. She removed her beanie and, ducking beneath the branches of the shrub, changed into the spare clothes she had brought with her and rolled on some deodorant. A splash of bottled water was all it took to remove the streaks of grass and mud from her face – her hair always looked the same whether she brushed it or not. Assuming an air of confidence, she emerged from the bush, strode to the front entrance and went in.

The automatic door swooshed shut behind her. The young man at reception smiled.

'How can I help you?' he said.

'I've come for an interview.' She folded her arms and gave him a petulant stare.

The young man – his badge said his name was Gary – looked her up and down. 'The interviews were earlier this week. No late entries.'

Gary was about eighteen and very handsome – and, to Jac's annoyance, his good looks were making her lose her nerve. She put her hands on her hips, but couldn't think of anything to say. She was about to annoy him by pressing the 'delete' button on his computer keyboard when the lorry driver came in with a large box and some paperwork to sign.

'This needs to go to the Principal's office,' said Gary, initialling the delivery note. 'Take the lift to the first floor, second door on the right.'

This was exactly the information Jac needed. Before the delivery driver could respond, she bolted away from the reception desk and into the lift. Gary shouted and chased after her, but the lift doors closed before he reached her. She waved cheekily at him as the lift rose up inside its glass tube.

As soon as the doors opened again, she ran to the Principal's office and barged in. Without saying hello, she addressed him with fire in her voice.

'My name is Jac Stryder-Jones and I want to be considered as a late entry into JASMINE.'

The Principal leant back in his chair and folded his chubby fingers across his stomach. 'Do go on,' his eyes seemed to say.

'I know I've got what it takes. I can write things that will change the destiny of this planet forever. When my final portfolio is published, the world will never be the same again.'

Still the Principal did not say anything. He took off his half-moon glasses and cleaned them with his handkerchief.

'I've seen things!' shouted Jac. 'I've got a stunning

story to tell and I will not rest until I've told it. I can bring this country to its knees and shock it back to life again.'

The Principal tapped his lips to conceal a smile. Who did he think he was, laughing at her like that?

'And I've been recommended by Penelope Steele at St. Philomena's,' she shouted, 'so you'd piggin' well better let me in!'

Tears were threatening to choke her voice, so she fell silent. The Principal raised his eyebrows, but nothing more. He turned his computer screen round so Jac could see it, and clicked the mouse. Grainy footage from a night-vision security camera appeared on the screen showing a shadowy figure falling over in the flowerbeds and crawling under a bush.

'Is this you?' said the principal.

Jac nodded. She wanted to die.

There was a knock, and Gary walked into the room – just in time to see the footage of Jac emerging from the bush.

'Is everything all right?' he said, stopping to stare as the CCTV film went round on a loop and Jac fell flat on her face again and rolled over in the dark.

The Principal waved Gary away with a quick flick of his hand. As soon as the door had shut he stopped the security tape and took a long look at Jac.

'Penelope Steele, you say?'

Jac nodded again.

'And you think you can produce a portfolio that will shake up this country?'

'Completely change the world,' said Jac.

The Principal looked at Jac for a long time, and drummed an insistent rhythm on the desk with his fingertips. Finally, he stopped tapping and picked up the telephone.

'Can I ask you to wait in Reception?' he said. 'Gary will get you a cup of tea, coffee; whatever you prefer.'

'If you insist,' said Jac, and she stalked out of the room.

Gary watched her come down in the lift.

'Principal says you should get me a cup of coffee.'

'Does he, now?' He leant his chin on his hand and stared at her, his warm brown eyes co-ordinating with his cool, gelled hair. He seemed to know that if he sat there long enough, being totally good-looking, Jac would melt away and never ask him anything again.

'All right, don't get me one, you goof,' she said, shrugging like she couldn't care less.

He pretended he hadn't heard her. He reached down below the desk and produced a cup of coffee and a bacon sandwich.

'Figured you might want breakfast.'

Without saying 'thank you', Jac tore huge lumps off the sandwich with her teeth and chewed noisily.

'Were you brought up by wolves?' said Gary. 'You're like a little feral kid.'

Jac pulled back her top lip to reveal a chunk of half-chewed bread and bacon, and sneered disgustingly at him.

Gary laughed and swung from side to side on his chair. After a while, the phone rang. It was the Principal, and he asked Jac to return to his office. She made a point of ignoring Gary – who was still watching her and smiling – and went up to the first floor.

'Sit down,' said the Principal. 'I've spoken to Miss Steele, and we both agree that your unavailability for the initial interview was extremely disappointing.

However, when I told her of the events of last night and your … emotional speech this morning, we are prepared to make an exception in your case. You have shown the determination and commitment that we want in our students. We have decided to allow you to begin the application process. But this does not mean that you will be given a place on the course. In fact, I have to tell you, that your portfolio will have to be twice as good as the other applicants for us to consider you worthy of a place.'

He downloaded something onto a memory stick.

'Take this,' he said. 'It contains everything you need to know about your first assignment, and what to do after that.'

The email alert sounded on his computer, and he glanced at the screen.

'You must go,' he said. 'Do not contact JASMINE until your portfolio is completed.'

He clicked on the mouse, and already engrossed in his mail, waved her out the door.

XIV

JASMINE
assignment one

KEYWORDS:

authority
disguise
hidden
truth

your deadline is april 30th @ 12 noon

IT IS ESSENTIAL THAT THIS ASSIGNMENT IS KEPT SECRET UNTIL YOUR COMPLETED PORTFOLIO IS SUBMITTED ON JULY 21st

XV

Jac's bedroom wall had become an enormous mind map. Sticky notes in four DayGlo colours were linked together with strands of wool held up with Blu-Tack. Every JASMINE keyword had been brainstormed, workshopped, gap-filled, rolestormed … you name it, Jac had done it.

But nothing was working for her. She had absolutely no idea what to write about.

She flopped backwards on her bed and checked her brand new smartphone. She hadn't heard from Fabian for five days. He hadn't even replied when she sent him a text to tell him JASMINE had given her a second chance.

This is weird where are u?

She waited five minutes. No reply.

R u ok?

He didn't respond.

If u r ok get back to me YOU PIG

She decided to get herself a drink, and went to the kitchen. When she opened the fridge, a jar of anchovies rolled out and smashed on the floor, sending glass and fish everywhere. She found a dustpan and brush and swept it up. There was a pile of old newspapers in the corner, and Jac took some to wrap up the mess and throw it in the bin.

On one of the front pages was an article about Richard Masters, the ex-Prime Minister. It was written the day after he had burst into tears and collapsed during Prime Minister's Questions. He was rushed to a mental health hospital, and soon after was transferred to a high security psychiatric unit. The report said he had become depressed when the British public had rejected his 'SuperSavings' campaign to cut back on spending. At the time there had been riots in the streets and calls for him to resign. The words in the article were cruel, calling Masters 'weak', 'pathetic' and 'a failure'.

Jac's heart raced like a rocket. The key to her assignment was right here, in these few centimetres of newsprint:

The ex-Prime Minister was once a symbol of **authority** (Check!)

He was **hidden** (Check!) from sight in a hospital in the middle of nowhere.

In his speeches, before he got ill, he was always talking about Britain having to accept the **truth** about saving money (Check!).

She tore out the article and ran back to her bedroom. Using a huge blob of Blu-tack, she stuck it right in the centre of the wall and trailed the wool from the keywords to the news story. As she re-routed the strands a final thought crashed into her head:

What if she used some sort of **disguise** (Piggin' CHECK!) to gain access to the hospital and interview him?

A man no-one would listen to … given the chance to speak – by her?

The idea was irresistible. And JASMINE would

have to be impressed.

She texted Fabian straight away:

I am a genius! Text this number to find out more!!!!!!

She waited, but he didn't get back to her.

XVI

Fabian finally phoned her nearly a week later, when she was sitting at Coventry railway station waiting for her connecting train.

'Hey, Jacs.'

'Hey.' She left a pause to see if he would explain why he hadn't called her, but he didn't.

'Congratulations on JASMINE! I salute you, fair maiden! Did you really spend all night in a bush?'

She was in a huff with him, but she didn't let on. 'Me and a dead bird. It was mega-skanky.'

'You around later? We could meet for a coffee.'

'I'm actually on my first assignment. I'll be out of contact for a while.'

'Oh, cool.'

He didn't sound bothered. She started counting to ten, giving him one last chance to say why he'd not been in touch. But before she'd reached 'five' ...

'So I guess I'll see you when we're back at school.'

'Yeah. Then we can swap news ... I want to ... hear your news.'

'Nothing to tell, sweet-pea.'

The public address system announced that Jac's train was about to arrive.

'Gotta go, Fabes.'

'Yeah, I heard. Good luck! Love you loads.'

'Love you, too.'

She dropped her phone in her bag and zipped it up crossly. As the train pulled away, she huffed to herself and wondered what the piggin' heck was up with him.

About twenty-five minutes later she got off the train at a remote village station. The taxi she had booked was waiting for her. There was a post box at the end of the station approach, and she asked the driver to stop for a moment. She took an envelope out of her pocket and held it in both hands. She had packed it full of European stamps and addressed it to Colette's home in Grimaud. She had written PLEASE FORWARD in several colours on the envelope, and the letter inside begged Colette to use the stamps, write to her and tell her that she was all right. Her fingers trembling, she got out of the car and released the letter into the black hole in the box. But, deep down, she knew that she would never receive a reply.

The driver coughed impatiently and Jac climbed back inside the cab. After twenty minutes she arrived at Stockbridge Secure Mental Health Facility.

It was an ugly building - a soulless cuboid of concrete that had been thrust on the surrounding countryside. It looked more like a prison than a place of care, with its cage-like railings and looped barbed wire snarling from the top of the perimeter wall.

As she walked towards the entrance, she saw a man in shabby pyjamas peering through a locked iron gate, gripping the bars as if he were afraid of falling from a great height. His head was cocked at an uncomfortable angle and he seemed to be staring at something on the ground, but there was nothing there. Jac approached him, but he didn't look up.

'Hi there?' said Jac.

The man rocked backwards and forwards without speaking.

Jac shifted uneasily. She needed to pretend she was visiting someone or they wouldn't let her in. 'Can you tell me your name?' she said. 'My name's Jac.'

The man continued rocking. It felt bad – very bad indeed – to be using this man to try and get access to the Centre.

'Jimmy.' Jac could barely hear the croaky, downtrodden whisper that leaked out of his mouth like a dying breath. 'Jimmy Johnson.'

'Hi, Jimmy Johnson.'

'Jimmy Johnson.' The man nodded as he spoke, but still he did not look at her.

This was awful.

Jimmy pressed his forehead into the railings as if he were trying to hurt himself.

Jac looked around for help. She didn't know what she was supposed to do, so she started talking. She pointed at the green area behind him.

'I like your garden. It's cool.'

Jimmy's eyes flickered, as if a thousand nasty memories were haunting him at once.

'Do you like this garden?'

An ant scuttled from the gate onto Jimmy's hand. Still with his head glued to the railing, he watched the ant out of the corner of his eye as it ran up his arm. 'Jimmy Johnson,' he said again. He lifted his head, his forehead now branded with a white, bloodless mark where the railing had been. A tear ran down his grey, dreary cheek.

Jac bit into her thumbnail and stared at her shoes. 'Well ... nice to meet you,' she said. Awkwardly, she walked away. She didn't look back.

She buzzed to be let into reception and told them she had come to visit her uncle.

'I'm here to see Jimmy Johnson,' she said, once she was inside.

The receptionist jabbed at the computer keyboard. She stared at the screen then looked suspiciously at Jac. 'There's no-one here with that name,' she said.

'Oh dear. Is he calling himself that again?' said a passing nurse. She smiled sympathetically at Jac and gestured to the receptionist that everything was fine. 'Poor old Ned; he never got over Jimmy's death, did he?'

Jac shook her head, as if she knew all about it. Inside her pockets, her hands sweated with relief.

'Shall we fetch him?' said the nurse. 'We can bring you tea in the lounge.'

'I think he'd rather stay in the garden. I'll meet him there.'

'Ah! That's sweet of you.'

'Where are the ladies' loos, by the way? I've forgotten.'

The receptionist pointed. After Jac had signed in, she headed for the garden, walking down the corridor and out of sight.

Jimmy – or, rather, Ned – was no longer at the gate. Eventually she found him, apparently with the same ant on his arm, tracing its movements with his finger and crooning to it quietly. Jac said hello, but he showed no recognition of her, and she walked on.

She searched the gardens for three quarters of an hour, hoping for a lucky sighting of Richard Masters – but that would have been too easy. Eventually she returned to the ground floor of the hospital and headed for the ladies' toilets.

Inside one of the cubicles, she took a white coat out of her bag and put it on. To the collar she attached a homemade ID badge, which said 'Bethany Jones – Visiting Therapist'. She tamed her curls with 'wet look' gel and pinned her hair back with Kirby grips. She went to the wash basin and put on some lipstick, scowling at her girly, dark pink lips in the mirror. A woman came in. Jac nodded professionally and the woman smiled back. She pretended to wash her hands, then set off to explore the building.

She had done her research on mental health care. Staff wages were low, organisation was poor and the nurses were overworked and stressed. Many staff left their jobs after less than three weeks. Jac was confident that, if she kept a low profile, people would either be too busy to notice her, or they would simply assume that somebody else knew who she was.

Only the ground floor of Stockbridge was open to the public. There were two lounges and a cosy cafeteria, and a conservatory that overlooked the gardens. They had tried to make it look like an old-fashioned hotel.

But on the upper floors – beyond the soft carpets, the pot plants and the beige wallpaper – a maze of starkly-lit passages snaked upwards and outwards, separated by creaking fire doors. Jac walked among the patients, who drifted like phantoms along the corridors and stood, sentinel-like, in bedroom doorways.

A shaky hand grabbed her and a wild-eyed man pleaded with her to make the bombing stop. He was so frightened even the hems of his pyjamas trousers were shaking. Jac had barely prised herself away when another man demanded directions to the Taj Mahal and threw his shoes at her when she said she didn't know how to get there. As she hurried free, she stumbled upon a woman sitting on the floor singing to a doll as if it were a real baby – and then, in the distance, a terrible, tortured wailing rang out and never stopped. Everywhere she looked, eyes pleaded, rolled and glared, fingers pointed and wringing hands clutched and trembled. It was too much for Jac, and she ran upstairs to a deserted landing.

At the far end was a locked door with a security keypad. A sign said:

'ACCESS STRICTLY PROHIBITED. SENIOR STAFF ONLY, TO BE ACCOMPANIED AT ALL TIMES BY THE MANAGER.'

There was a clipboard hanging on a hook by the keypad. Jac took it and traced her finger down the chart of names, dates and medication. On the second page she found Richard Masters.

She tried keying '0000' and '1234' into the keypad – sometimes even professional people got sloppy – but the door did not open. Frustrated, she peered through the square of wire-reinforced glass at the deserted corridor beyond. To the left and right, every one of the white, shiny doors was double padlocked and, at the far end, a security camera swivelled slowly.

The sound of footsteps came from behind. Jac searched for somewhere to hide, but it was too late.

'What the hell are you doing up here?'

Still clutching the clipboard, Jac turned around, her heart in her throat.

A tall woman in a navy blue suit was staring at her, and she didn't look pleased.

XVII

The woman's name badge said 'Liz Malhotra: Manager'. Her eyes narrowed, and she scrutinised Jac's fake ID.

'I think I got lost,' said Jac. She bit her lip, and waited.

'You certainly have,' said Ms Malhotra, taking the clipboard and returning it to its hook. 'Mrs Roe is on the first floor. Her reflexology was due to start ten minutes ago.' She gave Jac a stern glance and gestured impatiently. 'Come with me.'

As they walked down the stairs, the manager shot a sideways glance at Jac. 'You look very young,' she said.

'I'm seventeen,' said Jac. 'Everyone in my family looks young.'

'Lucky you.' Ms Malhotra did not smile.

Mrs Roe was sitting in a tatty armchair, and glowered when they walked in.

'Another new therapist this week, Elsie.'

Mrs Roe harrumphed noisily. 'Is she my daughter?' she said.

'No, dear.'

'Are you sure?'

'Yes.'

'Good,' growled Mrs Roe. 'I hate my daughter.'

'Bethany's going to give you a nice foot massage,' said Ms Malhotra.

'Bah,' said Mrs Roe.

As the manager closed the door behind her, Mrs Roe shook her fist and swore. She kicked off her slippers and socks to reveal a pair of scarred, twisted feet.

'Damned therapists! Bad eggs, the lot of you.'

An acrid, cheesy smell was rising from the old woman's toes. Jac reluctantly filled a bowl lying by the washbasin with water and washed Mrs Roe's feet with the soap from the dispenser on the wall. Mrs Roe's bones seemed to be jutting out in all the wrong directions and touching them was making Jac feel sick.

As she patted them dry with a towel, Jac remembered that reflexology wasn't just for feet. Francesca the PA used to give her a relaxing hand massage sometimes, then paint her nails for her.

'I'm going to do something a bit different today,' said Jac, rummaging in Mrs Roe's chest of drawers for a clean pair of socks. 'Here. Put these on. And leave those manky old slippers off. Let your feet breathe a bit.'

Jac pulled up the only other chair in the room and sat on it in front of Mrs Roe. She took hold of Mrs Roe's freckled hand and began to gently work the muscles.

Mrs Roe closed her eyes. As Jac transferred the massage strokes from the base of the palm towards the tips of Mrs Roe's fingers, the wrinkles on Mrs Roe's face seemed to dissolve away. Jac had thought she was about eighty, but maybe she was only sixty – or even fifty.

After a while, Mrs Roe started to hum to herself.

'You're a good girl,' she said, suddenly opening her eyes. 'I always told 'em. My little girl's a good girl.'

And she began to talk.

'Do you remember when I used to sing at the opera? I used to take you in your pushchair to the rehearsals. Good as gold, you were. They used to say you were my little angel.'

She crooned an aria from La Bohème, her eyes smiling.

'And they treat me well here. Although some of the others are very queer fish. But I don't keep with them.' She leant towards Jac and her voice became a proud whisper. 'Every week, I have a cup of tea with the Prime Minister!'

This was such a confused conversation – but could this be the bit where a poor old woman was telling the truth? Jac pulled Mrs Roe's hand towards her.

'The Prime Minister? When does that happen, Elsie?'

'Tuesday mornings ... Or Wednesdays. Or is it Friday?'

Jac squeezed the woman's hand tightly. 'It's Friday tomorrow. Is it Friday you see him?'

Mrs Roe didn't like the sudden change in pressure, and snatched her hand away. 'Get off me, you cow!'

'But your massage!'

You're only doin' it because you want my money!' The wrinkles returned to Mrs Roe's face, creeping across her skin. 'Go on, get out of here!'

There was an alarm cord in the corner by the bed, and Mrs Roe eyed it meaningfully.

'You're not fit to be called my daughter!' She

pointed at Jac and shouted as loudly as she could. 'Bugger off you stinkin' thief or I'll call the nurses!'

Before Mrs Roe could draw any more attention to her, Jac picked up her bag and fled from the room.

XVIII

'What's going on?' A nurse had come to investigate.

'Mrs Roe thought I was her daughter,' said Jac. 'I'm afraid I only gave her half her massage.'

'That's more than most people manage,' said the nurse. She looked at her watch. 'You need to go. Lockdown in fifteen minutes.'

Jac returned to the ladies toilet and hid in the same cubicle as before. She wiped off her lipstick and used more gel to make her hair look messy and greasy. She took off the white coat and undressed down to her underwear. After clipping a money belt round her waist and hiding her phone and her mum's credit card inside, she put on some pyjamas and an old pair of slippers. She hid her bag with all her clothes in at the back of the cleaning cupboard and stepped out into the corridor.

Immediately, the sound of an alarm bell reverberated through the building. The security camera at the end of the corridor turned on its base and pointed straight at her. Staff appeared out of rooms and offices, and rushed towards her, Liz Malhotra striding out in front. Jac shrank back against the wall as they came nearer, grasping feebly for an excuse to explain why she was now wearing pyjamas. But they swept past her, leaving a breeze in their wake.

She waited until they had disappeared, then walked to the abandoned front desk and signed herself out. The alarm stopped ringing and, as the sky outside the hospital grew darker, Jac headed for the second floor in search of somewhere she could spend the night.

There were two residents' rooms that appeared to be empty. One was on a landing between the second and third floors, and a thick, grey blanket had been left folded on a chair. Jac closed the door and played games on her phone until the lights went out. Then, drawing the rough, itchy blanket around her, she curled up on the bare mattress and tried to sleep.

The souls of the patients became more tortured after nightfall. As Jac lay in the dark, desolate cries and moans punctuated the black silence like wolves calling to each other across an empty forest. Every now and then, restless footsteps scurried across the floorboards outside the door, and in the distance, patients banged on the walls and muttered like ghosts. In the room next door, two sets of desperate fingernails scratched repeatedly at the walls.

Slowly, a sense of fear mushroomed through the building, the loud howls and sobs building to a crescendo. The footsteps stamped and clattered; the distant bangs and crashes got nearer and more intense. Jac got up, grabbed the chair and pushed it against the door, wedging the backrest under the handle. She returned to bed, curled tight, her hands clasped over her ears. Finally, at about three o'clock in the morning, a calm descended. No longer feeling threatened, she fell half-asleep.

The next thing she knew the chair was flying

across the room. It landed on the floor with a violent clatter. Someone came in, walked straight to the bed and shone a torch in her face.

'OK, OK, I'm sorry!' moaned Jac. 'I've been very stupid and I'll leave immediately!'

But there was no reply. Instead, a small hand reached out and stroked her hair. The light from the torch shifted from Jac's eyes and briefly illuminated the other person's face. A pale, waxy-skinned girl with pallid lips and greenish eyes was watching her carefully. She could only have been about seventeen.

'It's safe in here,' said the girl.

'Er, yeah,' said Jac, moving away from her.

The girl leant across the bed and, to Jac's horror, lifted the blanket and got into bed with her.

'Safe in here,' crooned the girl. 'Safe-in-here-safe-in-here-safe-in-here-safe-in-here-safe-in-here-safe-in-here-safe-in-here-safe-in-here …'

She cuddled up to Jac, soothing herself with her chanting, and playing with Jac's hair. Jac could feel the girl's pulse vibrating through her tiny, thin body, and her weak, shallow breaths as they blew on the back of her neck.

She lay, tense, not daring to move. She didn't like hugs at the best of times, but this was really creepy. After a while the girl fell asleep, and Jac realised that, for the first time since she'd gone to bed, she was feeling warm. The warmth brought with it a feeling of sleepiness; her body started to relax into the mattress, and – despite the fact that she was sharing her bed with an unstable stranger – she drifted into a deep sleep.

When she woke up at 9.00 a.m. the girl had gone.

As she stretched her legs along an empty corridor, a door to the left was flung open and a shriek of fury rang out, drowning out the words of a nurse who was appealing for calm. A plastic bowl of porridge was thrown through the doorway and it bounced off the opposite wall, congealed oats and milk sticking to the paintwork. Two pieces of toast and jam followed, complete with a plate; they too struck the wall and ended up, butter side up, on the floor.

Seeing and smelling breakfast made Jac realise how hungry she was. She hadn't eaten since lunch the day before. Without thinking, she picked up a slice of toast and started to eat it. The nurse saw her, but had clearly seen similar behaviour before and said nothing. Stuffing her face, Jac shuffled away down the corridor.

She found Mrs Roe downstairs in the lounge and watched her from a distance, turning her head away whenever a member of staff passed. At half past eleven, a nurse patted Mrs Roe on the shoulder.

'Guess who's coming to have a cup of tea?'

'Is it my daughter?' barked Mrs Roe.

'It's a VIP,' whispered the nurse.

Mrs Roe chuckled with delight, and the nurse took her to the conservatory. Jac followed, and waited. Eventually a man with wispy hair and a checked cardigan was brought in and he sat down beside Mrs Roe, grinning like the Cheshire Cat.

'Here's your Prime Minister,' said the nurse, winking at a colleague.

Mrs Roe gave a queenly wave and thanked the man for coming.

'Am I the Prime Minister?' said the man, still grinning. 'Ooh, how lovely.'

It was always going to be too piggin' good to be true. Jac sighed and turned her thoughts back to the rooms on the third floor and the locked door with the

83

keypad. She tried to think where she could hide up there, in the hope of discovering the access code.

A hand tugged at her sleeve: it was the girl who had climbed into bed with her the night before. She sat on the armchair next to Jac and clung to her. The girl laced her fingers around Jac's, pulled Jac's hand up to her mouth and began sucking both her own thumb and Jac's at the same time.

'Oh please don't do that,' said Jac, her stomach turning. She wriggled out of the chair, but the girl continued to grip her hand and kept trying to put it back in her mouth.

'Please – let me go,' whispered Jac.

At that moment Mrs Roe looked up and began shouting.

'It's her again! That thieving therapist who pretended to be my daughter!' She stood up and jabbed a finger in Jac's direction, attracting the attention of at least two members of staff. 'Look at her! She's disguised herself as a patient, the deceitful cow!'

The wispy-haired man roared with laughter at this revelation, and continued to laugh when Mrs Roe spat violently, sending a stream of saliva through the air. The nurses rushed forward – one towards Jac – and the paper-thin girl started to cry. Jac prised her hand free, and gently pushed the girl into the arms of the approaching nurse. She looked into the nurse's eyes and saw a look of suspicion; a look which said 'do I know you?'

'Wait,' said the nurse, but Jac had already turned away.

There was a crash as the tea tray went flying, and cries of 'get the knife!' as Mrs Roe turned her anger on the wispy-haired man. Jac was forgotten, and she rushed from the room, intent on taking refuge in the toilets. She swung round a corner, looking over her shoulder to check that no-one was following her.

As she turned back she crashed into someone. Somebody tall and strong. Somebody who instinctively cradled her to cushion the collision. Her face had smashed into his chest; she pulled her head back and looked up.

She was in the arms of Richard Masters.

XIX

'Are you all right?' said Masters.

Jac turned her face towards the wall as the nurse who had given her an odd look in the conservatory hurried past. Her heart was throbbing like a pneumatic drill.

'I'm not a patient,' she said breathlessly. 'I'm a trainee journalist. I've come here to interview you.'

Masters' expression changed. 'If you've come here to humiliate me ...' He gripped Jac by the elbows and pushed her against the wall. 'All it takes is for me to start shouting and they will have you restrained within seconds.'

'I'm not going to humiliate you!' Jac's blood raced through her body so fast she thought she was going to faint. 'I was in France two weeks ago! I know the truth!'

Masters' grip loosened.

'My friend Colette ... died because of it,' breathed Jac. She heard her voice crack, and Masters let go of her.

He rubbed his face with his hands. He surveyed the corridor and spoke in a low voice. 'Then you must come with me.'

He took her to the third floor, typed the security

code into the keypad and opened the door.

'They think I'm too messed up to notice the number,' he said.

He took her to his room: comfy, much nicer than the rooms on the floor below.

'They only let me out of here for an hour a day,' he said, looking longingly out of the window at the gardens. 'But we are safer in here.' He gestured to her to take a seat.

'You're very young,' he said.

'I'm still at school.'

'And you engineered all this …' He looked at Jac's pyjamas, '… to come and speak to me about what is really going on in Europe?'

Jac nodded, and Masters smiled.

'You're not as … ill as I thought you'd be,' she said. She pressed the 'record' icon on her smartphone.

'By 'ill' I take it you mean 'mad'?' said Masters.

Jac shifted awkwardly.

'I have severe depression,' said Masters, sitting down on his bed. 'It made me mad for a while, but now they've got my medication right I feel almost human … most of the time.'

'How come you got so ill?' asked Jac. Masters had been such a tough, charismatic politician until he became Prime Minister.

'I had strong beliefs,' he said. 'Britain is in deep trouble and I thought I knew how to put things right. We had to save money before the country went bust. I had faith that the people of Britain would understand what needed to be done – so I proposed a tough series of SuperSavings. But everyone went crazy. They wouldn't listen. They wouldn't let me do it. They put their love of luxury ahead of everything else.'

'The riots?' said Jac.

Masters nodded. 'Everybody said I was wrong. I couldn't understand it. The way I saw it, a huge tsunami was crashing towards Britain. I tried to warn everyone that there was no money left. But nobody wanted the SuperSavings to affect them. The tsunami came nearer … I warned them again … but even my own people told me to be quiet.' He buried his face in his hands. 'The Home Secretary was the worst. He said we needed to be popular, so we had to give people more money, not take it away.'

The powerful man who had held Jac in his arms had disappeared. Masters sniffed forlornly.

'I'm sorry – I don't have a tissue,' said Jac.

'No matter,' said Masters. 'Even *I* think I sound like a madman. Tsunamis, indeed!'

'You're not mad,' said Jac. 'I told you – I've seen the effects of the … tsunami for myself. In Saint Tropez … and Grimaud.' She shivered as a sickening slideshow of memories came back to haunt her.

Masters got to his feet. His strength had returned as quickly as it had disappeared.

'Then you see what has to be done?'

Jac nodded.

'But you're …'

'Fourteen,' said Jac. She cringed: she must sound like a jumped-up little kid.

Masters studied her face thoughtfully. *'Where there's a will, there's a way,'* he said eventually. 'I've always believed that.' He paced around the room, then gestured towards Jac's phone. 'Is that thing still running?'

They both looked at the little microphone icon

flashing on the screen. Masters washed his face at the basin in the corner of the room then returned to his chair.

'Then let's begin.'

He spoke for nearly an hour. He told Jac everything he believed must be done to save Britain from ruin.

'You must never stop talking about this, Jac. But like a dripping tap. Not too much. That's the mistake I made. Just little bits of information, nagging away at people until they start to understand the truth.'

He named people he thought might be allies, and those – including the Home Secretary – who were his enemies. He described his SuperSavings policies in detail: everything he had planned to do if he had stayed in office. By the end his charisma filled the room; he spoke and gestured like a great orator. When he stopped he stared at Jac, shocked to remember that he had an audience of only one person.

'Now that really is the first sign of madness,' he said. 'Delusions of grandeur.' He tapped the side of his head as if to say 'See, I am insane after all'.

Jac touched the smart screen and turned off the voice recorder.

'I'd make you a cup of tea but I'm not allowed a kettle,' said Masters. 'All that hot water and electric wire: too dangerous. But they do trust me with a packet of biscuits. Would you like one?'

As he moved towards a cupboard in the corner, the noise of distant police sirens could be heard outside. But instead of passing, the whoop-whooping got louder, until there was a screech of tyres on the tarmac and the sound was immediately below them.

Masters and Jac went to the window. Four police officers got out of two cars, and one of them approached Liz Malhotra who was waiting on the driveway. They began to talk. Beside Malhotra was the nurse who had recognised Jac in the conservatory earlier. She too was talking – quickly and with urgent gestures ... and then she handed something to a second officer. It was the bag Jac had hidden in the cleaning cupboard.

The officer studied the photo on Jac's fake ID; another came over and rummaged through her clothes. There was a short discussion and the officers ran towards the hospital entrance.

'Listen to me,' said Masters. 'There's a fire escape at the far end of this corridor. A few yards from the bottom of it is a shrubbery, which will give you cover, and beyond that is the tradesman's entrance. The keypad code for the door is 7565; it's never been changed.'

He took her hand and held it in both of his.

'Do you have money?'

'Card,' said Jac.

Masters walked to the door, opened it and listened. Jac joined him. There were footsteps running up the stairs to the third floor. At the other end of the corridor, a pair of police boots climbed the fire escape.

'I thought they'd do that,' said Masters. 'But I will get you out of here.'

Jac felt sick. How would she possibly escape now?

The footsteps had reached the security door and it beeped as the key code was accepted. At the other end of the corridor, the door to the fire escape crashed open. Masters walked to a drawer and took out something small and shiny.

He spoke quickly but with complete calm. 'You must trust me now. What I am about to do is something I have done before. I do it in such a way that I don't come to any ... harm. Please don't be upset. Just seize the opportunity to escape when you see that the time is right.'

Footsteps approached rapidly and stopped in the doorway.

'And, Jac ...' His eyes misted again. 'You need to find a way to make the people of this country listen. Drip, drip, drip. Before it's too late.'

He kissed her hand and gestured to her to stand by the door. A second later it swung open and hid her from sight.

'Come out of there!' shouted Ms Malhotra. 'We've seen the CCTV footage and we know you're in there. You will save yourself a lot of trouble if you give yourself up quickly.'

From behind the door, Jac could just see Masters. She watched him use a razor blade to inscribe deep cuts across the veins in both wrists. Large, syrupy drops of dark red blood fell instantly and splashed into the carpet. Jac felt sick and looked away.

Malhotra, another member of staff and two police officers rushed in. Masters fell to the floor so that his arms were beneath his body – and it took all four of them to turn him over so that they could administer first aid.

Behind them, Jac slipped out of the door. As she ran away down the corridor, she heard a female police officer radio urgently for an ambulance.

The metal stairs clanked softly under her slippers as she ran down the fire escape. Once in the shrubbery, she steadied herself amongst the leaves. As soon as the nauseous ringing in her ears had subsided she staggered to the tradesmen's entrance, keyed in the code and – pulling her pyjamas tightly around her – pushed open the heavy wooden door and stumbled out into the street.

XX

A noise woke Jac at six thirty.

Finding herself in a sitting position, she thought at first she was still in the taxi that had taken her from the Stockbridge Institute to the railway station three days ago. She pulled herself upright, expecting to see the driver staring quizzically at her pyjamas in his rear-view mirror. But then she remembered she had been at her desk all night. She rubbed her face, and felt the imprint of the computer keyboard on her cheek.

She hadn't finished editing her JASMINE assignment about Masters, and the deadline was today. Why was it proving so difficult to write, when it was such a simple thing she wanted to say?

She had a shower, got dressed and went to the kitchen. There was a slice of takeaway pizza in the fridge, left over from the night before. She ate it cold and rushed out of the front door.

Not long afterwards she was striding through the protest camp. It was twenty past seven. She was determined to complete her report before registration.

Richard Masters' suicide attempt was still all over the papers. Some of the protesters had made Richard

Masters masks, and had photoshopped letters across his forehead spelling the word 'LOSER'.

How could they be so cruel? Jac snatched a can of cola from her schoolbag and shook it hard. She primed the ring-pull, preparing to spray the drink everywhere and soak the masks. But the protesters laughed.

'Ooh – fizzy pop! I'm terrified.' The man with the *'Kiss Me, I'm Too Poor to Buy You Flowers'* T-shirt spurred his mates to join in. 'Little Miss Posh-Face wants to cola-ize me!'

With a snap, the ring broke off in Jac's hand.

'Ha ha! She can't even get it open!'

'Help! It's a dumb kid with a broken can!' A woman stepped forward, sneering. As a sick joke, she had daubed red paint or ketchup across her wrists, and had let it run gruesomely down her arms and onto her clothes.

In fury, Jac threw the can as hard as she could, and it struck the woman on the head. A deep cut peeled open above the woman's eye and she fell to the ground. Real blood glistened as it mingled with the fake red splashes on her T-shirt.

For a moment the protestors stood, stunned. Then a shouting mob rushed forwards, stumbling through the tents and sleeping bags, screaming insults and trying to see where they were going through the holes in their masks. Jac turned and ran as fast as she could towards the sanctuary of the school.

The corridors were calm and almost empty. For a moment, Jac leaned against the wall to catch her breath, and then she walked on.

She found herself sharing the school with people she normally avoided: swots heading for the library, girlie girls huddled in cliques, geeks going to maths club and nerds – well, just being nerds, as far as she could see. It was a whole new world. But she liked the peace of it all. It felt safe.

A Year Eleven girl overtook her, MP3 earphones stuffed into her ears. She had a badge on her schoolbag: a tribute to American pop star, Anson Perry. Most of the girls were mad about him – but Jac thought he was a goof. The girl was singing – badly – to one of Perry's songs.

'Imagine a world where nobody asks for more,'

Jac pranced behind the girl, flapping her arms stupidly.

'Where everyone knows what it really means to be poor.'

Jac opened and shut her mouth like a goldfish, lip-syncing with the lyrics:

'If we all hold hands, and the singers and bands
Ask the world to stop acting like one ... big ... shiny ... Superstore ...
Then maybe – just maybe – we can open the door (the door of sanity!)
And pick ourselves up off that greedy, needy floor (farewell to vanity!)'

The Year Eleven girl missed the high note by a mile, and Jac stuck two fingers into her mouth and pretended to be sick. Seeming to sense Jac's presence, the girl turned round. Jac skulked up the stairs and out of sight.

Halfway up she bumped into Fabian. He was deep in conversation with a boy from Year Nine, the two of them leaning against the banister, mirroring each other's body language as they talked. The younger boy was like a negative image of Fabian: his pale blond curls and big, oval grey eyes the exact opposite of Fabian's near-black hair, and eyes and skin the colour of dark chocolate.

'So – what's the big secret? Anything I should know?'

Fabian blushed and took a step backwards. The other boy smiled.

'Since when have you come in so early?' said Fabian, his cheeks taking on a deeper tinge of pink.

'Since when have you been hanging out with scrappers?' said Jac. 'No offence,' she added, grinning at the Year Nine boy. 'Does the scrapper have a name?'

'Freddy's from drama club,' said Fabian. 'He's playing Brutus opposite my Caesar.'

'*I kiss thy hand,*' said Freddy, taking hold of Jac's fingers and pressing his lips against them, '*... but not in flattery ...*'

'... But not at all, thanks very much,' said Jac, pulling her hand away and wiping it on her jumper.

Freddy's big, pale eyes sparkled hypnotically, and Jac looked away.

'I ... should go,' said Fabian.

'Sure,' said Freddy. 'Later, though, yeah?' He picked up his bag and walked down the stairs.

'Seeya, weirdo,' called Jac. 'Good luck with the play.'

Freddy turned, blew a kiss and slipped away round the corner.

'What's with his eyes?' Jac grimaced at Fabian. 'They're ...?'

'Amazing?' said Fabian.

'Freakish,' said Jac.

'Amazing ... for an actor, I mean,' said Fabian. 'They're very expressive.'

'Well, don't stare at them too long – you might go mad and kill the Headmaster.'

Fabian looked at his watch. 'Can we get a drink in the common room? I need to talk.'

'Sorry,' said Jac. 'I have to finish my JASMINE report. Can't stop.'

Fabian looked disappointed, and part of Jac was glad: she had finally got her own back on him for ignoring her during the holidays. But he did look hurt. She would make it up to him soon, she told herself. Buy him a smoothie at Mozelli's and have a BIG chat. Yes – they could talk another time.

At the English lab she plugged in her memory stick and carried on typing where she had left off. She was now more determined than ever to honour Richard Masters and get this assignment right, after the disgusting behaviour of those trolls at the camp.

'Hey! You're cutting it fine!' Miss Steele appeared behind her. 'That had better be good, young lady!'

She sounded jokey, which was annoying. Miss Steele had been pretty mean to her the last time they spoke.

'Well done on getting in, by the way.' Miss Steele winked meaningfully. 'I knew you had it in you.'

No you didn't, you chummy cow, thought Jac. She didn't like Miss Steele any more, and clicked the mouse so that her report disappeared from sight.

'You can keep your work on file here in school if you want,' said Miss Steele, squinting and trying to read the title of the document.

'No thanks,' said Jac. 'I'd rather do exactly what JASMINE says.'

'Sure.' Miss Steele patted her on the arm. 'But if you change your mind ...' She went to her desk, spent a few minutes at her computer, and then left.

'JASMINE will mail me your next assignment at

noon,' she called from the door. 'I'll pay you a visit after lunch.'

Jac resumed writing. She blocked out her irritation at Miss Steele's fake behaviour and edited the final paragraph. As she finally clicked 'Save', the registration bell went. She put the memory stick in her school bag and left the lab.

At lunchtime, Miss Steele handed her a white envelope. 'Assignment number two.'

Jac took it from her with a shrug, and Miss Steele walked away. Jac went to the girls' toilets, locked herself in a cubicle and tore open the letter.

She read it a couple of times, but before she could even start to think what to write, there was a loud knock on the cubicle door.

'Bog off,' she shouted.

Nobody spoke. A few seconds later, a half-eaten tuna wrap sailed over the toilet door and landed by her feet. Then a slice of tomato came skimming over and splatted against the cistern.

Jac flung open the door. It was Fabian.

'What are you doing, you maniac?'

Fabian grinned and flicked a bit of cress at her.

'You really are the world's goofiest berk, you great big ...'

'Goofy berk?' said Fabian.

A Year Seven girl came in, screamed at the sight of a boy in the girls' toilets and fled. Jac and Fabian doubled up laughing. Mimicking the girl's scream, Fabian clutched his cheeks with his hands and flounced out of the door. Jac chased after him, and Fabian ran down the corridor, screeching madly.

Mr Figgis appeared and gave them both a Friday detention.

XXI

Jac sneaked out of the detention room, leaving Fabian to write an essay on 'The Benefits of Silence' alone.

Since the cola can incident three days ago, she had been travelling on the tube to avoid walking through the protest camp. When she arrived at the tube station, the entrance was blocked. Four small girls were walking up the stairs, each carrying a bunch of helium balloons. Their party clothes and happy faces were of no interest to the other passengers, who grumbled as the children left the station.

'You're taking up enough room for a whole ruddy army with those stupid balloons,' said a man in a suit. The children's mother glared, and the angry commuters squeezed past them down the steps.

A busker got on the same carriage as Jac. To her annoyance, he started singing the same Anson Perry song that the Year Eleven girl had been listening to at school. Still, she only had to travel one stop and then she could escape. But the carriage was warm, she was exhausted, and the busker had a pleasant, lilting voice. She leant back in her seat, closed her eyes and decided to relax … just for a few moments.

When she opened her eyes again, the train had

reached the end of the line. The carriage was empty. Her mouth felt sticky and the shadow of a strange dream was lurking at the back of her mind.

She looked down and saw that she'd dribbled on her blazer. She wiped herself with a tissue, glad there was nobody there to notice. Then people started getting in again, and the driver announced that the train would soon depart. Passengers appeared in ones and twos, filing through the doors and choosing a seat. It was weird watching complete strangers gather in one place, united by a need to travel in the same direction. As the carriage filled up, remnants of Jac's dream crept back in to her head – and suddenly she remembered all of it.

With an excited heart-flip, she rummaged in her bag for her JASMINE assignment and re-read it. She realised that, whilst she had been hurtling through the tunnel towards the suburbs of the city, she had half-dreamt the solution to her next project. Ideas had been dancing around in her sleep and now they were a fully formed plan.

As the train pulled away and rattled along the darkened track, Jac scribbled some notes onto the back of the assignment envelope: Anson Perry's song – balloons – a group of strangers with a common direction ...

She couldn't wait to make her dream a reality. And she couldn't wait to see the response. It was just the sort of thing Masters had suggested – a drip-drip of information to get people thinking.

It was going to be amazing.

XXII

JASMINE
assignment two

KEYWORDS:

**public
message
network
authority**

your deadline is may 21st @ 12 noon

IT IS ESSENTIAL THAT THIS ASSIGNMENT IS KEPT
SECRET UNTIL YOUR COMPLETED PORTFOLIO IS
SUBMITTED ON JULY 21st

XXIII

Organising a flash mob was fun.

Jac climbed out of a taxi holding a box of personalised balloons. The cab driver helped her by carrying two canisters of helium gas to the front door.

'Havin' a bit of a party, then?'

'Sort of. Don't forget to pick up my friend, will you?'

'I'm on it. You kids behave yourselves!'

The cabbie drove away. Jac heaved everything inside and hid it in the wardrobe.

She still hadn't treated Fabian to that smoothie – she'd hardly seen him – so while she waited for him to arrive she opened the fridge and poured some Raspberry Riot from a carton into two tall glasses.

Twenty minutes later the doorbell rang. Fabian was wearing a new shirt and smelled of aftershave.

'Have you got them?' asked Jac.

Fabian pulled a bunch of keys from his back pocket and rattled them triumphantly.

'They were *so* easy to steal,' he said, pointing to a label attached to the keys that said *Queen's Street Offices*. 'They were dumped in a drawer in Dad's desk. They've been there ever since the Party moved to their new premises.'

He handed the keys to Jac and she turned them over in her hands, the different coloured metals plinking against each other.

'I had a look inside last night and nobody's been there for months,' continued Fabian. 'But the electricity's still connected. Typical government money wasting.'

Spotting the smoothies on the kitchen table, he walked off towards the kitchen to fetch them.

'I can't stay long, by the way,' he called.

'Before we start,' said Jac, 'I need to give you something.'

Fabian grabbed the smoothies and followed Jac into her bedroom. Jac pulled a baseball cap and a tracksuit from a carrier bag and waved them at him. 'If you're joining in,' she said, 'no-one must recognise you.'

'Crap goes the weasel!' Fabian gawped at the nylon trousers and top. 'I'm going to look like a chav,' he moaned.

Jac went to her computer and logged on to the fake 'SPREAD THE LOVE' page she had created on Best*Friends. A cheesy photo of Anson Perry smiled and waved at them from the screen, inviting fans to a new and exciting event.

'It looks great,' said Fabian. 'Really convincing.'

As Jac flexed her fingers over the keyboard, she ran the criteria for the second JASMINE mission through her head. There wasn't anything much more **public** than a flash mob. She certainly had a **message** – although she was disguising it as Anson Perry's. And she had used social **network** sites to organise the whole thing ...

'Come on, dreamer,' said Fabian.

———

103

Jac's fingertips tapped the keys. The new post was brief:

22, Queen's Street, SW1. May 18th. 12 noon.
Further instructions when you get there.
ANSON THANKS YOU FOR HIS LOVE.

Jac surveyed the screen and a ripple of satisfaction danced up her spine. After everyone had gathered at 22, Queen's Street, she was going to send her flash mob to Number One, Horse Guards Road, London. It was address of the Treasury – the place where every single decision about Britain's money had been made for the last thousand years.

She completed her JASMINE checklist: the flash mob was going to challenge the **authority** of the British government using a pack of teenagers, a load of balloons and a REALLY annoying song.

XXIV

Jac was dressed in her mum's pink velveteen jogging suit, a matching baseball cap and a blonde wig. Fabian looked worse in his tracksuit than either of them had imagined.

It was the day of the flash mob, and they were inside the disused government offices. In what used to be the waiting room, two hundred bright blue helium balloons bobbed against the ceiling, their ribbons hanging down like cooked fettuccine. Each one bore the slogan 'IMAGINE A WORLD'. In front of the balloons was a life-size cardboard cut-out of Anson Perry holding a set of instructions. Next to the cut-out was a table, and on the table was a bowl of coloured sweets. The instructions that Anson was holding read:

1. TAKE A SWEET!
- **RED** = YOU WILL LEAVE BY THE FRONT DOOR
- **BLUE** = LEAVE BY THE BACK DOOR & TURN LEFT
- **GREEN** = LEAVE BY THE BACK DOOR & TURN RIGHT
- **YELLOW** = LEAVE BY THE BACK DOOR & GO STRAIGHT ON

2. NOW TAKE FOUR BALLOONS AND **WAIT!**

3. FINAL INSTRUCTIONS AT 12.30, **SO LISTEN OUT**.

'Can we do a test run?' said Jac.

Fabian grinned, and disappeared into a small office at the back.

'OK!' called Jac.

An Anson Perry ringtone chirped from a drawer in the table. Jac opened the drawer and answered the phone lying inside. Fabian spoke to her in an American accent:

'Time to go and spread ... the ... lurve!'

'Your destination is Number One, Horse Guards Road! Maps are provided. Please leave by your designated exit at thirty second intervals. Good luck! Anson is with you!'

The phone went dead. Fabian emerged from the office.

'How was I?' he said.

'Brilliant ...' But Jac couldn't disguise the dull tone in her voice. She flopped into a nearby chair. 'What if nobody comes?' she said.

'If Anson Perry told his fans to jump off Tower Bridge they'd do it,' said Fabian. 'They'll come.'

Jac looked at her watch. 'Half eleven,' she said. 'We should hide now in case anyone's early.'

She put the phone back in the drawer, and they went into the office and locked the door.

At five past twelve, people began to arrive. Girl-fans squealed; boy-fans whooped and laughed at the cut-out, the balloons and the sweets. From the level of buzz and chatter growing in the room, Jac reckoned there were at least forty people.

At half past twelve, Fabian rang the mobile phone in the drawer. The room went quiet. Whoever answered it put it on speakerphone and Fabian gave the instructions in his phoney accent.

Everyone did as they were told and, about twenty minutes later, the waiting room fell silent. Jac and Fabian let themselves out of the office. The sweets had been eaten and the wrappers dropped on the floor. The Anson Perry cut-out was missing.

'Crap – so's the phone,' said Jac.

There were about thirty balloons left; Jac and Fabian took four each.

'I can't believe that many came,' said Jac.

'Told you,' said Fabian.

'We'd better get out of here.' She put on a pair of dark glasses, and Fabian looked amused.

'You! Dressed up like pink trash, pretending to be a fan of the odious Anson Perry! Will you ever tell me what this is about?'

Jac smiled and shrugged. She left the building by the back door; Fabian by the front. As she emerged onto a busy London street she could see a trail of blue balloons bouncing ahead of her, seemingly coming from different directions and heading towards Horse Guards Road. People were staring, and some were following the balloons to see where they were going.

But her stomach lurched when she tuned the final corner and saw the Treasury building. A dozen police officers stood outside, and two of them were armed.

XXV

One of the police officers studied the balloons and spoke into her radio.

Her heart pumping, Jac ran to join the group. Then she saw a second gang of protesters. They were holding placards which said 'NO MORE GREEDY BRITAIN! THIS IS A RICH COUNTRY – BE GRATEFUL.' Nobody was taking any notice of them, and the police – who outnumbered the protesters by two to one – looked bored.

Fabian ran over to Jac. 'Watch this,' he said.

He approached one of the officers and told him that the flash mob was part of the 'Greedy Britain' protest. To Jac's amusement, one of the placard-wavers stepped forward and said that, yes, this was the rest of their group. The policeman nodded and marshalled the Anson Perry fans into position. The flash mob waved their balloons and immediately started singing. Looking very pleased, the six original protesters moved to the front of the singers and shook their placards at the passing traffic.

They were all attracting a lot of attention now. The balloons made the fifty-strong crowd look a lot bigger than it was, and the six 'GREEDY BRITAIN' signs waved defiantly in time to the music.

'Imagine a world where nobody asks for more,
Where everyone knows what it really means to be
poor ...'

The group swayed in unison and the song got louder and louder.

Jac smiled in relief: the presence of the other protesters had turned her flash mob into a proper, political event. Jac reckoned that most of the Anson Perry fans had no idea that they were taking part in a serious protest. It was quite funny, really. Fabian ran across the road and filmed it on his mobile phone.

Around them, cameras clicked and phones were held aloft to capture the spectacle of the flash mob. Cars and buses slowed down to watch; horns beeped and people cheered. The police officers spread out to manage the onlookers, as people gathered together and joined in with the song.

'THIS IS A RICH COUNTRY – BE GRATEFUL.'
'If we all hold hands, and the singers and bands
Ask the world to stop acting like one ... big ... shiny ...
Superstore ...'

A bunch of four balloons floated into the air, diffusing the sunlight in a soft sheen. They drifted past the windows of the Treasury and up above the rooftops, blending with the blue sky and disappearing from sight. *'IMAGINE A WORLD ...'*

A short while later, a second bunch rose into the air. And then a third. Two girls pushed their way out of the flash mob and walked away. Then a boy Jac recognised from school also left the group. What was going on? She hadn't given the signal to disperse yet. On the other side of the street, Fabian's body language showed that, he too, realised that not everything was going to plan.

Jac peered from left to right, trying to work it out. Another quartet of balloons drifted skywards. As the person who had released them hurried away, Jac saw a figure in a hooded top – probably male – moving amongst the mob. Every now and then, he stopped and spoke to one of the balloon-holders. His face was never visible – but the faces of the people he talked to suddenly changed. One by one, the teenagers became frightened, relinquished their balloons and left. Then one of the placard carriers slipped away, looking stressed.

Jac pressed through the mob towards the hooded intruder. Within seconds she was in touching distance, and she jabbed him angrily on the shoulder. He turned round, keeping his head dipped and his identity concealed.

'If you know what's good for you,' said Jac, before she had time to think, 'You'll leave *right now.*'

It sounded like something out of a bad gangster movie, but it seemed to work. The gatecrasher walked away. Furious, Jac pursued him. Fabian had already crossed the road and met Jac at the edge of the mob.

'I see we have a saboteur,' he said.

'You'll have to take over,' she said to Fabian. 'Give the 'stop' signal in a few minutes time. I'll see you back at the office.'

She shoved her balloons at him and hurried along the street. Ahead of her, hoodie boy turned left towards Parliament Square, where he dodged the traffic and scuttled to the other side of the road. As soon as he reached the safety of the pavement, he hurried towards Westminster Bridge. Jac followed him.

Halfway across the bridge, the stranger turned to

see if there was anyone behind him. Jac ducked behind an ice-cream booth, her heart zinging. She took off her tracksuit top and tied it around her waist, revealing an inconspicuous black T-shirt underneath. She removed her baseball cap and wig and dropped them into the Thames. Hoodie boy resumed walking, and so did Jac.

On the other side of the bridge she followed him across a busy intersection. He walked under the gloomily lit railway bridge by Waterloo Station, then took a right into a narrow side street. She followed him through another tunnel and into an industrial estate. On the left, were several business premises built into the arches under the railway line. Hoodie boy walked up to the fourth door. He pressed a buzzer, spoke into an intercom system and was let inside.

Jac walked past the door a few seconds later. She crossed the road, knelt down behind a parked car and pretended to tie her shoelace. Who was that boy? And why did he want to sabotage the flash mob?

A door slammed, and somebody came out of the block of flats next to the arches. Jac peered over the bonnet of the car – and an unexpected thrill of heat rushed to her cheeks. It was Gary, the receptionist at JASMINE.

She didn't realise he lived in London. He turned left and came towards her, his loose shirt (two buttons undone) rippling gently in the breeze as he strode along in his drainpipe jeans. Jac cowered lower behind the car, cringing with hot embarrassment. If he saw her dressed like *this*, she would die. She fiddled with her shoelace again, her fingers trembling. Gary's footsteps passed by on the opposite pavement, and eventually she could no longer hear them.

She stood up. The road was deserted except for a woman pushing a pram. She decided to return to Fabian at the government offices – hanging about would only draw attention to herself. She turned and took a long look down the street the other way, hoping for a last glimpse of Gary somewhere in the distance – but he had gone.

XXVI

Jac put her key in the front door and waved at Fabian as the taxi pulled away with him in it. After tidying up the government offices, they had swapped tracksuits for a joke, and Fabian gurned at her through the taxi window, his face surrounded with velvety pink. She laughed, pushed open the door and slipped inside.

Her parents' shoes were in the boot-rack by the front door. This was weird; they were never at home at this time of day, even on a Sunday.

'Get in the kitchen, Jacqueline. Now.' Her dad was standing at the far end of the hall, darkly silhouetted in the doorway. Anger spat between his teeth, and she did as she was told.

Her mum was sitting at the kitchen table. 'Darling! What *are* you wearing? You look like one of those awful children from the council estate.'

'Shut up Flick.' Her dad sounded almost murderous. 'We're not here to talk about fashion.' He pulled some photographs from an envelope and threw them onto the table.

Jac's heart nearly stopped when she saw what they were. Pictures of her waving a can of cola at the protesters at the camp; her throwing the can; the

113

woman protester slumped on the floor covered in blood; photos of the wound – cleaned up, stitched and bruised purple.

'There's video, too, darling,' said her mum. 'Everything caught on mobile phones.'

Her dad's lips curled. 'You stupid little girl. Some of our best clients are from that protest camp.'

Typical of my parents to support such foul people, thought Jac.

'Do you realise how much trouble we've gone to, to keep this quiet?' her dad continued. 'Luckily for you the protesters are so suspicious of the police they decided to come to their lawyers first.'

He banged his fist on the table, and some papers spilled out of a folder onto the floor. 'If this had gone to court … and got into the press, for God's sake! Thank God they never worked out that you're our daughter! Your little antics could have really damaged our reputation.'

This was probably the moment to say sorry, but Jac was distracted by the documents that had fallen out of the folder. There was a photograph of the Home Secretary – Fabian's dad – with a young woman.

'Are you listening, you ungrateful cow?'

'Yes – sorry,' said Jac. She daren't meet his eyes at first. Then she looked up slowly. 'Sorry Dad – sorry Mum. And … thanks … for sorting things out.'

Her dad snorted and poured himself a large whisky. As her mum picked up the papers, he took a large swig and it calmed him.

'And your mother's right. You look like a dragged-up guttersnipe in that suit.' He downed the rest of the glass in one. 'Now get out of here. Get your own supper after we've gone to bed.'

'Salmon quiche in the fridge,' called her mum, trying to be nice. Her dad banged the whisky glass on the table in irritation.

At ten thirty that evening Jac heard the clink of the drinks cabinet as her parents searched for something to wash down their sleeping pills. By ten forty-five they were in bed and both of them were snoring. Jac crept into her mum's office and searched for the file that her dad had knocked onto the floor.

The photo Jac had seen wasn't the only one. There were dozens of images of Fabian's dad with at least six different women. Jac leafed through them, her fingers trembling: the Home Secretary out to dinner with one woman, kissing another, fumbling with someone else in a darkened shop doorway. There were even pictures of him with a woman in his office ... it was horrible, embarrassing. And mortifying for Fabian, if he found out. Jac shoved the photos back into the file and read through the paperwork.

Someone had been blackmailing Fabian's dad, demanding half a million pounds to keep the pictures a secret. Otherwise they would sell the story to the newspapers and end the Home Secretary's career. Jac's parents had hired a private detective to find out some unpleasant things about the blackmailer. Then they had blackmailed *him* to keep quiet. And Fabian's dad was so desperate to keep his job that he was paying Jac's parents five times their normal rate.

Jac replaced the papers and left the file as she had found it. She walked into the kitchen and sat at the table, picking holes in the salmon quiche with a fork. How should she break the news to Fabian? *Could* she break the news to Fabian?

She tipped the quiche into the bin and ate half a tub of chocolate ice cream instead. Then she went to bed, her bloodstream buzzing with cocoa and sugar, and her mind whirling with unanswered questions about what to do next.

XXVII

Jac had managed to avoid Fabian for nearly a week.

Since she'd discovered the truth about his dad, she had gone in to school early and hidden in the English lab, using the time to write her second JASMINE assignment. Now the assignment was finished, she left home as late as she could, and hung around in the cloisters with the maths nerds right up until registration. Luckily, Fabes had been busy with extra drama rehearsals, and hadn't texted her since the flash mob. So she hadn't had to face him yet.

She had got up late that morning, and hurried to the tube station on an empty stomach. The ticket hall was busy, and she pushed through to the top of the escalator. She tried to hurry down the moving belt of stairs, but a tramp got in her way. She was just about to smack him in the legs with her schoolbag when he leant towards her and spoke.

'Good morning, Jac.' He had a French accent, and Jac stared at him in disbelief.

'What? You do not speak? Jean-Luc would be surprised to hear that his little firecracker has lost her voice.'

'How do you know Jean-Luc?' Jac's pulse raced into overdrive.

'There is no time for that,' said the tramp. 'After you left your hotel in Saint Tropez, Jean-Luc bribed a kitchen boy to find your address on the computer. I am here to pass on a message.'

'How? You're a liar,' said Jac. 'There's no internet or phone at Jean-Luc's place.'

'And you are a foolish girl. Do you think it is safe for Jean-Luc to communicate like that? This message has been passed from man to man and has taken many days to reach you. Now listen carefully.'

The escalator carried Jac and the tramp downwards, towards the dark web of tunnels that snaked beneath the city.

'Terrible news has reached us. An army – called God's Profiteers – is destroying Europe. They have already invaded Bulgaria and Greece. They promised the local people an end to their poverty – but only the invaders are getting rich. The Greeks and Bulgarians have been forced to work as slaves.

'God's Profiteers are devouring one bankrupt country after another. Soon they will take over Croatia, Italy, Germany, Belgium, France. After that, they will wait for Britain to go bust ... and they will gobble her up, too.

'It is vital, therefore, that Britain stays strong. The British government must be stopped from spending so much money. The only way to do this is to make sure Richard Masters and the SuperSavings supporters run the country instead. Here is Jean-Luc's message: *Do everything you can, Jac, to help us topple your foolish Prime Minister and his money-wasters. Britain cannot become slaves. We must stop God's Profiteers before they eat up the planet Use your passion. Make sacrifices. Remember Colette.*'

The escalator reached the lower level. The tramp

slipped away into the crowd and was lost from sight.

A tube roared onto the southbound platform. Jac pushed her way onto the train and found a seat.

This was mad. She was fourteen years old and a smelly tramp had just told her to bring down the British government.

She was really annoyed with Jean-Luc. Who did he think he was, playing at spies and making a big deal out of her part in all this? She was doing the best she could, wasn't she? She really believed she could change people's opinions when her portfolio was published ... but destroy the government? It was ridiculous.

The train slowed down and stopped, and Jac left the carriage. At the barriers, someone bumped into her. He was well dressed and in his thirties. His mini-tablet flew from his hand and fell to the floor, spinning across the tiles. Jac dodged the crowd and picked up the tablet, checking to see if it was broken.

It wasn't. To her astonishment, the screen was showing a web page about God's Profiteers – the army the tramp had just warned her about. There was another tab open and Jac brought it up with a tap on the screen: a forum on *dinkytalk* tagged *#greedyprofits*.

'I think I'll take that back now.'

The man appeared alongside her. Jac blushed as she gave him back the device. 'Sorry, I ...' she said.

'No problem, Jac. I think you have seen enough.'

With a rush of adrenaline, Jac realised that he, too, had a French accent.

The man turned to slip away, but the belt buckle on his coat got caught on a button on Jac's sleeve. He tried to tug himself free, but the two of them were locked together.

'Got you,' said Jac. She held her arm so he couldn't un-jam the button from the belt. 'Tell me who you are,' she said. 'And then I will let you go.'

'I cannot do that,' said the man, looking around him. 'But I will tell you this. You are not the only person to be given this message today. There are many of us. We are everywhere, trying to save Britain so that Britain can save the world. But it is not easy. Your stupid government is silencing every message coming from Europe. They have hundreds of people watching the Internet, ready to delete information before it can be read. It is almost impossible for our voices to be heard.' He tugged impatiently at the belt. 'We might be being watched. We must separate.'

Jac fiddled with the dark grey button. 'But what can I do?'

'You will think of something. God's Profiteers cannot be allowed to take over the planet.'

Jac worked the buckle free. Like a phantom, the man moved away and disappeared. His last words before he vanished were:

'We must expose the truth. *Hashtag: greedy profits.* Look it up before it gets deleted.'

Jac stood still, commuters swarming around her like ants. This was getting madder by the minute.

She pushed her way through the ticket hall to the newsagent's booth and bought herself a caramel bar and an apple for breakfast.

Glad to get away from the airlessness of the tube station, she walked along the street towards the school.

XXVIII

Fabian was leaning against the wall outside the school gates. Jac's heart sank. What if he already knew about his dad? She really didn't want to have an emotional chat about *that* right now.

'Who are you waiting for?' said Jac. 'The Fun Bus doesn't stop here.'

Fabian had no comeback. 'Hi,' he said, digging his hands deeper into his trouser pockets.

They walked across the school lawn in silence. Halfway, Fabian stopped. 'Can we talk?' he said.

Jac wanted to get to the English lab and look up *#greedyprofits.* 'I can't,' she fibbed. 'I've got work to do for JASMINE.'

Fabian turned his head away.

'How about later?' said Jac. She felt bad now. 'We could get a smoothie after school? My treat.'

'Can't – drama club.' The words snapped from Fabian's mouth.

'Well, I'm busy this weekend,' said Jac. It was another lie, but if Fabian was going to get stroppy, then his stupid problems could wait.

'OK – smoothie bar after school on Monday.' Fabian gave a toss of his head and walked off towards the Year Ten block. 'Half past four?'

Jac nodded, and watched him until he had disappeared. She was glad he'd gone.

She skipped registration and went straight to the English lab. Checking she was alone, she logged on to *dinkytalk*, and keyed in *#greedyprofits.*

A discussion was taking place as she read, and she used the 'translate' facility to follow it:

FatherAleksanderBoter @FatherAleksander
Bulgaria 2 seconds ago
How can a hungry man resist the promises of God's Profiteers? Yet we must imagine a world where the poor are not exploited. #greedyprofits

Bogdan @BoyBogdan *Croatia* 20 seconds ago
Is my country in danger? #explosions Some say an 'army of God' is grouping at the border. #greedyprofits

Selene @SeleneDemos *Greece* 1 minute ago
Street fighting now. #explosions 30+ dead already. WHO ARE THESE PEOPLE? THEY SAID THEY HAD COME TO HELP US. #greedyprofits

Selene @SeleneDemos *Greece* 2 minutes ago
There are soldiers in the hills. They are not from my country. #explosions

TahaniHakim @TahaniHakim *Libya* 2 minutes ago
African Intelligence Agency: Eastern Europe is under threat. Anyone out there confirm? #explosions

Before she could read more, the words started to distort. The web page buckled and warped, then shrank to the size of a postage stamp and disappeared. An error message showed on the screen:

```
Could\not\open\the\tagfile#greedyprofits
bleep\g18orb\473922C
No such file or netstream exists
```

Frustrated, Jac typed in *#greedyprofits* again. The discussion had completely disappeared. But twelve words remained in her head:

'Yet we must imagine a world where the poor are not exploited.'

That was what that Bulgarian priest had said, wasn't it, before his *dink* was deleted by the British government forever? She typed in *#imagineaworld* – and with a thrill she realised she'd hit the jackpot. Hidden amongst thousands of *dinks* from Anson Perry fans, there was a thread of conversation that the internet censors hadn't detected. And it made her heart flip.

DasWerewolf @WolfgangBraun
Germany 4 days ago
It was someone from London. I heard it was a kid.
#imagineaworld #flashmob

IrinaC @IrinaCristea *Romania* 5 days ago
This #flashmob gives us hope. Perhaps Britain will stand firm as it did in the Second World War #imagineaworld

GoranaA @goranaali Turkey 9 days ago
Hearing someone made a protest in Britain to stop the greed. Please God let it be true! #imagineaworld #flashmob IT'S OUR ONLY WAY OUT!!!
As she read, a new message came in:

JamesJonas @jimboJ   *UK* 5 seconds ago
Looks like there are more of us here fighting the cause.
Greed must end! #imagineaworld
#flashmob WHATEVER IT TAKES ...

A fluttering began in Jac's stomach and reverberated through her body. These people were talking about her! And they believed her flash mob had made a difference.

She stood up – and noticed with a rush of excitement that she felt taller. She walked over to the window and looked down at the street, then out across the city. She wasn't alone and powerless, after all.

There were people out there trying hard to change the world. The 'dripping tap' Masters had talked about was working. Maybe, if they all pulled together, they could actually stop Europe disintegrating.

She wanted to be part of it – and for the first time, she really believed she could do it.

XXIX

'Assignment three.'

Miss Steele had found Jac in the cloisters before registration on Monday.

'Here.' She handed Jac a sheet of paper. 'You can look at it now, if you want.' She glanced at the maths geeks huddled nearby. 'How do you feel it's going?'

'Great, thanks,' said Jac. She unfolded the paper, and a shiver rippled through her. Two of the keywords – **expose, sacrifice** – had been spoken to her at the tube station three days ago. 'Has JASMINE been talking to some Frenchmen?' she joked.

'What?' Miss Steele's voice sounded suddenly tense. She moved nearer, her face dark. 'What did you say?'

'Just messing,' said Jac. 'Sorry.'

Miss Steele eyed her sternly. Jac tried a smile and it seemed to work.

'Hmm. You always were a cheeky gal. Speak to me like that again, though, and I'll give you detention. Understand?'

Jac nodded – although she thought Miss Steele was being seriously weird. She re-read the JASMINE brief and frowned.

Miss Steele spoke again. 'They tell me the competition for JASMINE is strong this year,' she said. 'There are others who might beat you to it. May I give you some advice? Take a risk. Take a big risk.'

She patted Jac's arm meaningfully.

'Put your neck on the line. At JASMINE they like that.'

A classy ringtone rang out from Miss Steele's pocket. She felt for her phone and answered it. As she walked away, she smiled at Jac and mouthed the words 'take a risk' again.

The registration bell rang. Jac folded the piece of paper in half and went to her classroom.

*

It was twenty past four, and Jac hadn't seen Fabian all day. He didn't turn up for registration and they had been in different classes after that. She walked out of the school gates, stopping to check that she had enough money to pay for two smoothies.

As she crossed the road, she noticed someone sitting in a van wearing overalls and a cap. It looked like Gary from JASMINE. With a frisson of excitement, she walked up to the passenger window.

It was him. She tapped on the glass and pulled a face. 'What are you dressed like that for?'

Gary gestured to her to get in.

'My mum told me not to get into cars with strangers,' said Jac.

'Just hurry up!' Gary looked bemused. 'You're drawing attention to me.'

Jac climbed in. 'I'd be embarrassed, too. You look like a Chuckle Brother.'

Gary smiled. 'I guess I do.' He looked at Jac's school uniform. 'I forgot you were studying here.'

The cab of the van was small, and Gary's long legs were only thirty centimetres from her own; his left arm just a touch away. Jac's heart fluttered inside her chest, and the scent of Gary's aftershave made her feel giddy.

'So – did you get fired, then?'

'No. This is my other job. I'm part time at JASMINE until September.'

'What do you do?' This close up, she could see the freckles on his face.

'Handyman. Didn't you read the side of the van?'

Jac shrugged.

'Some journalist you'll turn out to be!'

'At least I'm not dressed like Super Mario.'

'At least I don't sleep under bushes and eat like a pig.' His brown eyes sparkled, and Jac felt a thrill of heat spread across her cheeks.

'Have you been working in school?' she asked.

'Just finished. In the staff room putting up shelves.' He checked his watch. 'I'm ... waiting for my girlfriend now, actually. In fact ...' He started up the engine. 'She's late. I'm going to have to drive round again. I'm out of time on the parking meter. Can I drop you off somewhere?'

'Forget it,' said Jac.

There had only been one word in that last sentence: *girlfriend*. Her heart sunk like a stone.

She clambered out of the van. Gary nodded goodbye and drove away. Jac hurried towards the tube station.

She was so annoyed with herself. She hated the fact that Gary made her have ... feelings. Feelings were dumb. Feelings made you need people. And when you start needing people, they always hurt you.

She kicked a drinks can into the gutter and told herself she didn't care that Gary had a girlfriend. He was just a smarmy receptionist-handyman in baggy overalls who drove a crappy old van. He was nothing to her – she was fine. But the nasty, stinging feeling refused to go away.

When she reached the tube station a man dressed as Shakespeare handed her a leaflet advertising a play.

'No thanks, beardy,' she said. 'I get enough of actors at school with ... oh, PIGGIN' HECK!'

She shoved the leaflet into the man's chest and raced back up the road towards the smoothie bar. She checked her watch as she ran: it was ten to five. Her feet pounded the pavement as she dodged the stream of people heading for the tube station. Damn, damn, damn! She had really let Fabian down.

When she arrived at Mozelli's she stopped outside for a few moments, gasping for air. Inside, she could see Fabian at their favourite table with his back to her. She had decided she would act surprised when he told her about his dad. She went in, and the little bell on the shop door tinkled melodiously. Hearing the ringing sound, Fabian turned. His eyes looked watery.

'I'm so sorry,' breathed Jac.

'Where have you been?' His voice sounded spoilt and demanding.

'I met someone, I ...'

'To do with JASMINE, I suppose.'

Jac thought of Gary's long, slender limbs, so close to hers. 'Sort of.'

'I knew it!' His voice was too loud now, and

people were looking round. 'You've really changed since you got involved with them. *JASMINE this, JASMINE that!*' He spoke the last words in a mocking, whiney voice. 'That's all I hear about! The only way I get to spend time with you is if I help you with your stupid tasks. What about me, Jac? I've been trying to talk to you for ages.'

She'd felt sorry before she arrived, but the silly, emotional voice and the comment about her assignments annoyed her. She snapped back at him. 'I've been really busy – you know that.'

'Something happened last week and I've been desperate to talk to you about it.'

'I'm here now!'

'Too late. You should have been thinking about me earlier, instead of your portfolio! What about how *I* feel for once?'

This was rich. 'You tell me how you feel every piggin' day, Fabian! JASMINE is the first thing I've ever done that makes me happy, and you should be pleased for me. How about *my* feelings?'

Fabian flicked his head to one side. More tears grew in the corners of his eyes. 'You don't have any feelings,' he shouted. He stalked off through the tables towards the exit.

Jac stood still; the door slammed and the bell jangled across the awkward silence. Everyone was staring at her.

A waitress came and cleared away Fabian's empty smoothie tumbler. The clinking of the glass on the tray broke the hush, and people returned to their conversations.

'You'll make up, don't worry,' said the waitress as she passed.

'Are you a psychologist?' asked Jac.

The waitress smiled and said she wasn't.

'Then shut up,' said Jac, and walked away.

The air outside did nothing to soothe her anger and hurt. For the second time that afternoon she walked to the tube station in a blur. The man dressed as Shakespeare tried to give her a leaflet again and she told him to bog off.

She strode down the escalator and waited impatiently for a train, pushing in front of other passengers as soon as the doors slid open. The train had barely moved off when a piece of chocolate biscuit looped through the air and bounced off her cheek. A couple of feet away she saw Rufus, chewing and sneering at the same time.

Jac looked away scornfully, took hold of the handrail and closed her eyes. A whirl of thoughts engulfed her: Gary and his dumb girlfriend, Fabian's pathetic moods ... Fabian's sad, disgusting father. She breathed in and, once again, told herself she didn't care, pushing her feelings away, deep inside her where they couldn't hurt. Making a huge effort, she turned her mind to other things: JASMINE, Miss Steele's pep talk about taking risks – and her next assignment ...

Another piece of biscuit landed on her. From the sticky stain it left on her lapel, it was clear that Rufus had sucked it first. She looked over and thought how odious he was.

As the train rattled through the darkness, an idea hit her like a bullet. She realised she had everything she needed for her next assignment. Not only would it be high-risk, and seal her place at JASMINE, but it could damage the government, too – just like Jean-Luc and Richard Masters wanted. This morning, she would never have dared to do it – but now Fabian

130

had been horrible to her, she didn't care about the consequences.

She stayed on the tube until Rufus's stop and followed him up and out into the suburbs. She tapped him on the shoulder and, plunging her emotions way, way down beyond the depths of her heart, she told him she needed his help. With a steady voice, she explained to him that she wanted to ruin the career of the Home Secretary.

Rufus had never looked more pleased.

<u>xxx</u>

JASMINE
assignment three

KEYWORDS:

expose
secret
authority
sacrifice

your deadline is june 11th @ 12 noon

IT IS ESSENTIAL THAT THIS ASSIGNMENT IS KEPT
SECRET UNTIL YOUR COMPLETED PORTFOLIO IS
SUBMITTED ON JULY 21st

XXXI

A foggy drizzle hung in the air, and the light from the street lamps floated like balls of golden candyfloss against the night sky. It was the first of June tomorrow, but it felt like February.

Jac stood outside Opposition Headquarters in Westminster Street, the night porter watching her through the glass panels in the door. She pulled her beanie hat further down over her ears, the damp wool scrunching beneath her fingers.

A man in a raincoat shuffled past, dragging a sodden spaniel on a lead.

'Evening,' he said.

'Hi,' said Jac. Her voice sounded raspy, tense, unused. With a sinking heart she realised that she had barely spoken in two weeks. Her parents were at a conference in America, she never talked at school unless she had to – and Fabian had done everything he could to keep away from her.

Her phone rang: it was Rufus.

'You there?'

'I've been here ages. You're late.'

'Didn't want to come out in this filth unless you'd turned up. See you in five. Ciao.'

Jac dropped her phone back into her pocket.

Inside, the porter picked up the handset on his desk and made a call.

Since her big row with Fabian, Jac's anger had cooled. She had decided not to expose the Home Secretary's affairs with women – it would be too cruel, to hurt Fabian's family like that. But from what Richard Masters had told her, there would be other scandals to unearth in Fabian's dad's emails. And who better to help her dig around than the son of a top civil servant who worked for the opposition party?

Rufus arrived fifteen minutes later, in a silver Ferrari driven by his brother. He got out, and the car sped off.

'Hi,' said Jac.

Rufus didn't reply, and hurried towards the shelter of the Opposition HQ porch. He buzzed to be let in, and Jac followed him.

'Good evening, Master Rufus.' The night porter tipped the peak of his cap.

'Good evening, Long. My friend here will need a visitor's pass. Papa's given it the OK, as you know.'

'Of course, Master Rufus.'

Jac gave her details and the porter got the pass from the safe.

'Rotten weather, eh, Long?' said Rufus.

'Glad to be inside, young sir. And if I may say so, Master Rufus, you kept the young lady waiting in the rain rather a long time.'

Rufus snorted at the word 'lady', then checked himself when Long raised an eyebrow. 'Yuh. Pretty bad form, actually. Not like me at all. Yuh.'

Long asked Jac to sign the visitors' book.

'Would you like me to bring you tea and biscuits presently, Master Rufus?'

'No thanks. We'll fix it ourselves.'

'Right-o.' Long smiled at Jac. 'Hope you get what you need for your project, Miss.'

Rufus gestured that he and Jac should take the lift. As they stood waiting for the lift door to close, Long lifted his cap in respect.

'Sad old tosser,' Rufus sneered, as the door slid shut. 'So eager to please. I hate that.'

'You really are a complete turd,' said Jac. 'And an idiot. What do you think you're doing? Getting me to sign in at the desk? I told you I had to do this in secret.'

'And so you shall,' said Rufus.

The lift doors opened again and Rufus led her along a corridor with a rich red carpet. A CCTV camera followed them as they walked.

'Don't try and hide your face,' said Rufus. 'Act like you're meant to be here.'

Rufus let himself into his father's office and closed the door. He logged on to the computer whilst Jac fidgeted and eyed the flashing red light on the camera in the corner of the room. Rufus was leaving a trail as obvious as orange footprints in the snow and she wanted to give up and leave.

'OK ...' said Rufus. 'Now, do exactly what I say.'

'Why?'

'Because I'm doing you a big favour. Sit there.' Rufus pointed to a large leather chair.

'Why?'

'Just sit. Get your notebook out and write. Try to act less weird than normal.'

'Is this a joke?'

'Do you want to go home? Otherwise just do what I say.'

Jac shrugged, and pretended to jot something

down.

'Now look at me and say something without smiling.'

Jac looked up. 'You're a shrivelled piece of snot with a face like a dog's buttocks.'

'Hilarious,' said Rufus. 'Now say something else, but smile and laugh a bit.'

'You're a snotty piece of dog's buttock,' Jac said. She laughed fluffily. 'With a shrivelled up face.'

Rufus pretended to laugh back. 'You are such a pathetic cow. Now go back to making your stupid notes.'

Jac bit her lip to suppress a smirk and wrote 'Rufus is a willy' in her notebook. She still had no idea what was happening, but this was turning out to be weirdly fun.

'Now go and make some tea,' said Rufus.

'*What?*'

'Don't look at me like that, weasel mouth. Pass a cup to me, and stand next to me and talk for a while. Then sit down, drink your tea, chat, make notes, then get up and return the cup to the tray.'

'If you say so, dog breath.'

Rufus continued to issue instructions for about ten minutes, finally stopping to work at the computer. Jac got up and wandered round the room.

'Done,' said Rufus. He handed Jac a red key and pointed towards a black box on a shelf in the corner.

'Insert this into the control hub. Then, when I tell you, turn it clockwise.'

Jac put in the key. Rufus typed in a password.

'Now!' he said.

The image on the computer screen split into sixteen different segments, each one bearing a CCTV image of different areas around the building.

'I'm fixing the cameras on a loop,' said Rufus, 'so they will show empty corridors, even when we're moving about. Dad uses it when he wants to leave the room, unnoticed.' He tapped the mouse. 'See? Here's the film of us. The software takes the images and randomly edits them, so it looks like we're still here, working. When we won't be here at all.'

How did Rufus know all this stuff?

'Time to go,' he said.

He led Jac through a fire door to the back stairs. They descended several flights, finally reaching the lower basement.

It was full of bric-a-brac. Discarded chairs – most of them expensive, none of them broken – old lamps, a billiard table with a ripped baize, boxes of unfashionable champagne goblets and some ugly, oak furniture. Rufus pushed an ancient, dusty piano to one side, revealing a small door.

It had a computerised lock. Lights flickered on a control panel and its polished steel surface looked out of place amongst the junk. Rufus keyed in a code; a series of locks whirred and clunked deep within the door itself. And then the whole thing – about half a metre thick – swung open without a sound.

Jac thrilled with curiosity. Rufus – for some freaky reason that she didn't understand – was turning out to be far more useful than she had ever thought possible. She pulled off her beanie hat and ran her fingers through her hair.

Beyond the door was a dimly lit tunnel, musty-smelling and cold, stretching out into the distance before curving like a python and disappearing into the darkness beyond.

XXXII

Jac and Rufus walked in silence. The tunnel was almost circular, the walls arching upwards from the floor and meeting to form a curve just a few centimetres above their heads. Metal pipes and thick wires in assorted colours ran either side of them, bolted to the wall with giant staples. Apart from the odd fire extinguisher, there was nothing in the tunnel that made any part of it look different from the last. It was difficult to tell how far they had come.

'What are all these wires?'

'Electrical stuff. Telephone, fibre optics, cable TV. When the tunnels were built they disguised them as utility ducts. Hence the water pipes, too.'

'Wow – that is *so* interesting,' said Jac. She smiled to herself: she knew she could get Rufus talking in the end. Once he was in 'show off' mode, it would be difficult to get him to stop.

'Oh, yuh. There's a whole network of tunnels under London. All top secret, of course.'

They passed a hatch in the wall.

'See that?' said Rufus. 'Leads to an abandoned tube station. Greycoat Street. Was meant to be part of the District Line, but it never opened. The spy network used it in the Second World War.' He left a dramatic pause. 'I expect you're wondering how I know all this.'

Jac smiled.

'I use these tunnels quite a lot actually. Special permission from Her Majesty's Civil Service.'

'Your dad?'

'Yuh. You can visit every government building using these tunnels. Dad's people do it all the time. They've been stealing information for years. The politicians don't know, of course. 'Keep the thickos in the dark', that's what dad says.'

The tunnel broadened into a squarer, brighter space.

'Dad sends me down here on errands. When he needs to be seen somewhere else.'

There was a door, and another black box on the wall. Rufus inserted a key. Jac guessed he was rigging the CCTV in the building ahead of them.

'Yuh – he's given me loads of responsibility over the years,' continued Rufus. 'Says I'll grow up to be the best senior civil servant in the country. He'll be *so* impressed when he hears that I helped get rid of Barnaby Traves.'

The door swung open, and they stepped into a dark passageway. They walked up two flights of stairs, and through another door into a plushly decorated corridor. There was a familiar-looking logo on the wall, and a thrill bubbled over Jac's skin. She was in the Home Office. The Home Secretary's rooms could not be far away.

Footsteps approached.

'Security guard!' breathed Rufus, and they darted into the men's cloakroom opposite. They listened, waiting for the footsteps to fade away. But they got louder, and a group of three or four men came right up to the cloakroom – and Jac and Rufus were forced to retreat into the men's toilets behind.

'Damn! Must be a big drinks reception here tonight,' muttered Rufus.

The men laughed as they hurried through the cloakroom; Rufus ran to hide in one toilet cubicle and shoved Jac towards the other.

'There are only two loos in here, you goof!' hissed Jac. 'What if someone wants to use one?'

She followed Rufus into the cubicle on the left, bolted the door and sat on the toilet seat so that her feet were out of sight. Rufus hung back, looking uncomfortable.

Jac gestured that he should move away from the door. 'Nobody poos from there, you twit!'

Rufus moved right up to the toilet, turned his back on her and planted his feet self-consciously apart. The skin on the back of his neck was purple with embarrassment.

The men stayed for what seemed like ages. One of them lit up a cigar and, by the time they left, the room had filled up with sweet-smelling smoke. Rufus sniffed his designer cashmere jumper and frowned. 'Come on,' he said.

He led Jac through a network of back stairs to the office where Fabian's dad worked. He used a magnetic swipe card to gain access, then logged on to the computer.

'We don't have much time,' he said. 'Too many people wandering about.'

'Email account?' said Jac.

Rufus tapped in a password and the Home Secretary's email page appeared on the screen.

'It's that easy? Is nothing secret?'

'Not really,' said Rufus. He walked over to the

door to keep watch.

Jac inserted a memory stick into the computer. Whilst she waited for the files to download she decided to type 'God's Profiteers' into the document search window. She couldn't believe it when a large folder appeared on the screen. It was entitled 'GOD'S PROFITEERS – GLENOUSTIE CROFT.'

Rufus swore loudly. 'Get down!' he hissed, diving behind a filing cabinet.

A man and a woman were right outside the door. Jac ducked below the desk.

The pair outside talked breathlessly. With a nauseating squelch of her stomach, Jac recognised the man's voice: it was Barnaby Traves, Fabian's dad. The door handle turned, but the door wouldn't open. The Home Secretary tried the handle again a little harder – and then again. He muttered something about a faulty key card, and the woman suggested they went to her office instead. A few moments later the corridor was silent again.

'That's it,' said Rufus. 'We're leaving. Now.'

He went to the door to see if they were clear to leave. 'Come on,' he said.

'No – wait. Do you know anything about a place called Glenoustie Croft?'

'Never heard of it.'

Jac climbed out from under the desk. The email files had downloaded, but she wanted to copy the God's Profiteers folder. 'How come Traves couldn't get in?' she asked.

'I multi-locked the door from the inside. One more try and he'd have opened it. Dirty old man. The woman was Sir Kendrick's secretary. She's only twenty-two.'

Somebody else came down the corridor and Rufus

fidgeted. 'It's like a ruddy supermarket out there. You must leave that and go.'

'In a minute.' The God's Profiteers folder was only fifty-eight per cent downloaded and Jac shook her head impatiently.

'Come on,' said Rufus.

Jac ignored him. 'You don't seem surprised about Fabian's dad. The woman, I mean.'

'Everybody knows,' said Rufus.

There was an ominous click behind them. A portion of the wall moved slowly sideways. Pale light leaked through from another room behind.

'OMG – nobody uses that door,' said Rufus. His face looked sweaty and he shifted nervously from one foot to the other.

It was too late to hide. The wall opened up to reveal another office suite behind. But neither Jac nor Rufus were paying any attention to that.

Fabian was standing in the doorway.

XXXIII

There was a long silence as the three of them looked at each other, then Jac and Rufus spoke simultaneously.

'Look what the cat dragged in,' said Rufus.

'What are you doing here?' asked Jac.

'Shut up.' Fabian glared, half-furious, half-stunned, at both of them. 'I'm allowed to be here. My dad works here.'

Rufus laughed at the word 'work'.

Fabian looked slowly from Jac to Rufus and back again, and then to his dad's computer. His face went white.

'Oh, I see,' he said.

Jac felt a drop of cold sweat dribble down the back of her neck.

'You traitorous cow. Teaming up with *him*! Just to get some crap on my dad for your precious portfolio. Very nice. Very you.'

Jac avoided Fabian's gaze, and silence returned to the room as if a ghost had walked between them. Rufus sat down and swayed his chair from side to side, eyeing Fabian with a mixture of amusement and contempt.

An error alert chimed from the computer. Jac's

download of the 'God's Profiteers – Glenoustie Croft' file had been denied. She thumped the desk in frustration, removed the memory stick and put it in her pocket.

'And still all she cares about is getting her story!' Fabian's voice trembled. 'You really are a piece of work, Jacqueline Stryder-Jones! Cold like your mother, callous like your father.'

He must have known that was the cruellest thing he could have said. But he was right. Her voice cracked as she struggled to reply.

'Right now, my parents are actually *helping* your dad!'

Fabian eyes burned with disbelief.

Rufus, meanwhile, was casually cleaning his nails with one of the Home Secretary's business cards. 'Talking of your dad ... Were you looking for him?' he smirked. 'Because I know where he is.'

'Rufus, don't!' said Jac.

'Only, I expect you haven't seen him for a couple of nights,' said Rufus.

Fabian's anger was punctuated by a look of surprise.

'Now, let me see,' continued Rufus. 'Tuesday night he would have been at the Beresford Hotel with the Defence Minister's daughter. Wednesday is random date night, so he would probably have been at the Belle Vue. And tonight he'll be on Sir Kendrick's desk with the lovely Miss Soames. Third floor, last office on the left. No doubt he'll be pleased to see you. I'm sure he's missed you – and all the family.'

Fabian's face twisted painfully as he tried to come to terms with what he had just heard, and Jac's heart crumpled.

After a long pause, he spoke.

'And this – this is the story you've been grubbing around for? Your best friend's dad is a love rat?'

'No!' said Jac. She tried to make the whole thing sound unimportant. 'Everybody knows about it already.'

A gasp fell from Fabian's mouth. 'And that's supposed to make me feel *better*? Mum doesn't know! Jonas doesn't know! They'll be ...'

'Nobody cares,' said Rufus.

In a fit of fury, Fabian strode across the room and swung at Rufus with his fist. 'I thought I told you to shut up,' he said.

'Oh, get over it, gay boy!' To avoid the punch, Rufus spun round on the chair, grinning carelessly.

Jac told Rufus to stop being an idiot.

'But he *is* gay,' said Rufus.

'Do you have to be such a prat?' said Jac.

'He is. Ask him.'

'Don't be pathetic.'

But Fabian's face changed again. With a zinging heart, Jac realised that it was true.

All the anger evaporated from Fabian's face. He looked pale, lost, afraid – and exhausted.

'I've been trying to tell you.' His voice was barely audible. 'I was scared you'd ... But you're always too piggin' busy.'

'And now Frilly Freddy's finished with him and he's all glum,' jeered Rufus.

'Leave him alone!' Jac turned and looked at Fabian's stooping body. 'Freddy? The scrapper? With the spooky eyes?'

Suddenly it all made sense. Why hadn't she seen it before? All that disappearing, the moodiness, the embarrassment. She should have noticed. She *would*

145

have noticed. If she hadn't been ... No wonder he had been so angry with her at the smoothie bar.

Fabian's shoulders heaved. Jac wanted to hug him and say sorry, but she couldn't move. She felt awkward in front of Rufus and didn't know where to start.

Rufus stuck out his bottom lip and pretended to wipe away tears. 'Boo-hoo,' he said. Jac kicked him.

'Fabes ...' she said.

Fabian looked up. 'I know – I disgust you,' he said. 'Just like I disgust him and half the people at school.'

'They're idiots,' said Jac.

Looking lonely and broken, Fabian turned and left the room.

'What a pathetic little drama queen,' said Rufus.

'Drop dead, you goof.' Her heart pounding, Jac hurried towards the adjoining office.

'I don't care, Fabian – I don't care about it.'

But Fabian had shut the door and was gone.

XXXIV

After she and Rufus parted company, Jac went to an off-license and used her civil service pass as ID to buy a bottle of gin. Swigging from it to numb the pain of the meeting with Fabian, she walked into an all-night internet café and inserted the memory stick containing Barnaby Traves's email files into a computer.

She clicked on message after message. A conversation finally caught her eye: it was between Traves and the Commissioner of the Metropolitan Police, Sir Martin Wade. Sir Martin had written first: *'Barnaby – crime figures have dropped again. Your policies are working. The richer you make people, the less they want to break the law!'*

Barnaby Traves agreed ... but the words he used were dynamite. *'That's right! Keep the greedy little morons happy and they won't give us any trouble. I never realised governing Britain could be so easy! ...'*

Greedy little morons. Three words that would bring the Home Secretary's career crashing to the ground. Jac took another gulp of gin, and a heat wave of courage seared through her chest. In an email marked 'urgent' and 'explosive', she leaked Traves's ill-chosen comments to an online news agency. Then she sat in the corner and waited.

As the minutes dragged by, she ticked off the keywords on her JASMINE assignment, one by one. She had just **exposed** a **secret** conversation between two men in **authority**. Check ... ... check ... ... check.

Her pen hovered over the final word on her list, and she swigged another mouthful of gin. This time it made her feel sick. Would the **sacrifice** she had just made ever be worth it? Her actions had lost her the respect of her best friend. Forever. Check ...

An internet news channel picked up the story first. The tagline 'HOME SECRETARY 'MORONS' INSULT – MILLIONS OFFENDED' suddenly appeared in a strip at the bottom of the screen. And then it spread across the media like a plague. The television news channels caught the story, and the scandal blared from the TV in the corner of the café. Then it started trending on social network sites. By daybreak, the story would be on the front page of every newspaper. Jac got up, kicked the gin bottle under her chair and walked home.

She crawled into bed and slept fitfully. By the time she woke up at 9.00 a.m., both the Home Secretary and the Chief of Police had been sacked.

Jac was glad it was the weekend: for the next forty-eight hours, she didn't have to face Fabian. She wouldn't have to look him in the eye ... and see exactly how much he hated her.

She pulled the duvet over her head and wished the weekend would never end.

XXXV

The printer chugged monotonously, churning out sheet after sheet of identical sticky labels. Jac sat on the floor in her pyjamas, watching the paper slide rhythmically into the tray. Nine hundred and fifty down; another fifty to go.

Behind her, the television was on with the sound down. For the past hour, the news channel had been showing the disgraced ex-Home Secretary returning home after a fortnight's holiday in Wales, in a blaze of camera flashes.

She turned to face the TV screen. She watched Fabian's dad push his way through the mob and disappear into his house. The sideburns of his jet-black hair had gone suddenly grey, and his tall, robust frame seemed to have shrunk. A spasm of pain stabbed her heart as the camera strafed to a downstairs window where, briefly, Fabian's little brother Jonas could be seen peeping sadly through the curtains.

Fabian had been off school since the scandal broke. This was the second weekend Jac had spent alone, and the printer finished its job with a loud clunk. Jac checked the sheets; they were fine. JASMINE had sent her details of the next assignment three days ago, and the stickers were to be her new weapon to try and make the country change its mind about the SuperSavings.

There had been changes already. Since Barnaby Traves's email went viral, nobody wanted to be seen as 'greedy' or a 'moron.' Pool Prisoners had announced that it was closing down. The leader of the Better Bedcovers Movement had resigned. On a daytime talk show, the host had cut up his credit cards on air.

Jac switched off the TV and computer and changed into a dark pair of leggings and a hoodie top. She looked in the back of the wardrobe for the baseball cap that Fabian had worn on the day of the flash mob, and pulled it down over her hair. Putting the labels in a designer carrier bag, she headed out to catch a bus to Oxford Street.

As the bus lurched through the Saturday traffic, Jac took off the cap and turned it over in her hands. She lifted it to her face and breathed in. It still smelled of Fabes: a faint whiff of whatever posh soap he used. She thought of him in the disused government offices, larking about and singing a mad duet with the cardboard cut-out of Anson Perry. And then she remembered him walking away from her at the Home Office: stooped, hurt and alone.

The bus jarred to a halt and a solitary teardrop fell from the corner of Jac's eye and rolled down her cheek. She brushed it away, stared determinedly out of the window, and focused on the next mission.

XXXVI

JASMINE
assignment four

KEYWORDS:

message
authority
money
question

your deadline is july 2nd @ 12 noon

IT IS ESSENTIAL THAT THIS ASSIGNMENT IS KEPT
SECRET UNTIL YOUR COMPLETED PORTFOLIO IS
SUBMITTED ON JULY 21st

XXXVII

The ground floor of Fossingham's department store on Oxford Street was an extravagance of polished mirrors, cream-coloured marble and chrome. A multi-scented vapour hung in the air, as heavily made-up women in white jackets promoted perfumes, creams and lipsticks.

A girl selling fake tan looked at Jac, then turned away. They always did that; Jac just wasn't their type. She pulled the baseball cap over her eyes and moved through the displays, ignored and unnoticed.

She reached into her carrier bag and peeled off one of the labels. As she passed a shelf of expensive beauty gift sets, she slipped the label on to one of the boxes and walked away. She continued prowling the ground floor, unpeeling two or three labels at a time and sticking them on as many luxury products as she could:

Where is all your money coming from?
It's true: Britain is going BUST

A security guard looked towards her, so she took the escalator to the second floor and pretended to be interested in clothes that she would never wear, pressing labels onto sleeves, belts and collars. She visited each department in turn, posting her message on toys, designer cookware, top-of-the range handbags and over-priced pet accessories. Finally she took the lift to the basement and labelled some garden furniture. Then she left the store.

Dodging between the tourists on the street, she visited fast food chains and coffee shops. She sneaked stickers onto tables, menus, a baby's pram – and once, even the till.

Then she saw a glitzy gift shop and sauntered in. As she roamed through the mishmash of statuettes, candlesticks and trinket boxes, she spotted somebody shoplifting. They were very slick, pocketing a mobile phone case here; a pair of earrings there. Jac guessed that whoever it was could only be about thirteen.

The thief turned sideways, revealing a strand of light blond hair between his turned-up collar and polo cap. His skin was soft and pale, his eyes a smoky grey. Jac couldn't believe it: it was Freddy. Freddy the scrapper; Freddy as in Fabian's Freddy.

On the far side of the shop a sales assistant stared then spoke into a walkie-talkie. Jac coughed loudly; Freddy looked up and she caught his eye. She raised her eyebrows in alarm and nodded towards the other side of the store. Freddy put his head down and moved towards the exit. The store assistant strode after him.

'Stop right there!' shouted a security guard, but Freddy wove his way into a group of Japanese tourists and was lost from sight.

'And the girl, too! She's in on it!'

The shop assistant changed direction and swerved through the displays towards Jac. Paralysed for a moment, Jac watched him accelerate towards her.

Then, following Freddie's lead, she, too, shoved her way into the gaggle of Japanese shoppers.

'Excuse me!' shouted the assistant. 'Make way!'

The tourists were slow to respond, and Jac wriggled between them and burst free the other side. The exit was ahead of her – but it was blocked by two security guards.

'We've already called the police,' shouted somebody.

A strong hand gripped her arm from behind, twisting it backwards so she couldn't move. Someone put their face close to her ear and spoke harshly, their hot breath leaking onto her cheek.

'You need to come with me, you thieving little madam.'

XXXVIII

There was a loud crash as a two-metre-tall display of glassware cascaded to the floor. The woman who had grabbed Jac yelled in pain: part of the display unit struck her hard as it fell. Jac ducked out of the way, unharmed.

The guards at the exit rushed forwards. Jac felt a small hand slip around hers: Freddy was at her side. He looked at her, his big, almond-shaped eyes shining.

'Follow me,' he breathed. He pushed over another display and the two of them ran across the shop, the alarm bells inside the store clashing with the wail of police sirens outside.

They dodged through the shelves and burst through a fire door into a small yard. There was a wheelie bin nearby; Freddy grabbed it and they used it to block the door. The exit gate was locked, so they climbed over the top.

'This way,' said Freddy, and they fled up a side road away from the noise of Oxford Street.

After they had run four blocks, Freddy stopped, gasping air into his lungs. Jac leant on his shoulder, waiting for her muscles to stop hurting.

'We can walk now,' said Freddy. 'They never

chase this far.'

They continued for another block then turned down a narrow street. The buildings were tall and thin, and they had basements, boxed in with iron railings.

Freddy stopped outside a closed-down health clinic. He took off his hoodie, rolled it up and pressed it onto the spear-like points of the railing. Like a cat, he pulled himself over the top and dropped effortlessly onto the ledge the other side.

'Your turn,' he said.

Jac looked up and down the street. There was nobody about. She hoiked herself over the ironwork and landed next to Freddy.

The concrete floor outside the boarded-up basement was two metres below them. Freddy grasped the bottom of the railings and lowered himself until he was dangling by his fingertips. He let go and dropped silently to the ground. Jac copied him, her feet stinging on impact.

There was a padlock keeping the wooden boards tightly closed around the window. Freddy took something out of his pocket that looked like a thin knife with a kink at the end, and inserted it into the lock. It clicked and fell open. He peeled back the weathered sheet of wood and climbed into the room beyond. Jac followed him; Freddy replaced the board and closed the window behind them.

'You just saved my neck,' he said.

Jac shrugged, and looked round the tiny basement room in which she had found herself. The whitewashed walls were adorned with rugs, prints and arty photographs. Some of them looked like they were from the gift shop they had just been in. Two old armchairs had been draped with chenille throws, and an antique hat stand stood in the corner.

Freddy switched on a trendy-looking floor lamp and soft light spilled into the room. There was a kitchenette at the back, and he filled a kettle and found a jar of hot chocolate. Jac sat down on one of the chairs, picking up a carved wooden bird from a nearby table.

'You didn't steal *all* this?' she said. There was even a microwave oven and a mini fridge.

'I'm addicted.' Freddy grinned, spooning generous piles of chocolate powder into two mugs. 'My psychotherapist says it's a hoarding mechanism borne out of an unfulfilled need to be comforted, thanks to an absent father and an over-dominant mother.' The kettle chirped to the boil and he looked like he couldn't care less about his criminal habits.

'You're insane,' said Jac.

She returned the bird to the table and sank backwards into the chair, taking the hot mug from Freddy and breathing in the rich smell of cocoa. It was hard to relax when everything she could see, smell and touch had been shoplifted, so she closed her eyes.

When she opened them, Freddy was looking at her.

'Can you not do that?' she said. 'It makes me feel weird.'

Putting his elbows on his knees, and his chin in his hands, Freddy leant forward and stared even more. Jac threw a cushion at him to make him stop.

'Leave off, frog face!' she said. But really she liked it. It was exactly the sort of thing Fabian would have done to cheer her up.

A prick of pain came from somewhere. She thought of the confrontation with Fabes in the Home

Office ... and what she had done to his family ... and felt sick.

'Fabes is really upset that you two have split up,' she said, changing the subject. 'What happened?'

Freddy looked at the floor. 'It started with the stealing,' he said. 'Fabe said I should stop. But I don't want to. So I said he was just as bad as me because he wouldn't tell people the truth about our friendship. We ended up having a huge row.'

'But you want to get back with him?'

Freddy nodded. 'He said some mean things to me, though.'

'He does that,' said Jac. Her stomach twanged. 'But you should make up.'

Freddy said nothing and stared into his mug.

'I feel awful that he couldn't tell me about you two,' she said.

Why was she telling Freddy *that*?

'Just because Rufus is a pig doesn't mean I was going to be horrible about it,' she continued. 'But I shouldn't have been so busy.' She chewed her thumbnail. 'I know I can be a hard-hearted cow...'

Did she really admit that out loud? Freddy blinked his big, pastel eyes and smiled softly. 'Don't worry, I get it,' he said. 'You're messed up, like me.'

'Thanks a bunch, scrap-face.'

'D'you want to know what Fabe says about your parents?' said Freddy after a moment. 'He says they treat you like dirt and that it's amazing you're not some sort of mental case.' He gazed at her like an angel. 'He's always been worried about you.'

Jac took a cushion and hugged it tightly. 'But now he detests me.'

'He loves you,' said Freddy. 'That's why he hates you right now.'

Jac slipped off her trainers and curled her legs underneath her. Why was she telling this cherub-faced, spooky-eyed freak her innermost thoughts? It was baffling. But it felt OK.

'Could you let him know I'm sorry?' she asked. 'I don't think he'll let me talk to him. Tell him I've messed up. And tell him that him being gay makes sense and now I love him more than ever because ... I *get* him better?'

Freddy said he would.

'And make up with him at the same time.'

'Yes, mother.'

Freddy put his mug on the table. 'Do you like retro punk?' He slotted a top of the range MP3 player into a speaker station. 'Fabe hates it.'

A tortured guitar riff wailed across the room and the rough voice of the lead singer of The Screaming Puppies attacked the first verse. Jac hugged her knees and laughed.

'Yes, he does,' she said. 'But *I* love it.'

XXXIX

Jac typed the closing paragraph of assignment four, her fingers flying over the computer keyboard.

She was pleased with the way she had met the brief. Her sticky labels had sent a **message** that raised **questions** over the government's **authority** to handle **money**. She liked the neatness of it: the whole assignment encapsulated in a thousand rectangles of self-adhesive paper.

Her phone beeped. There were two messages.

Check this out, you messed up cow!
screamingpuppies.com/deadpixiemashup

She thumbed her reply:

Leave me alone you bug-eyed freak :)
already heard it anyway
(is awesome though) x

Another beep.

Ooh she sends a kiss! Love u too head
case x

Very funny.

Well I don't love you ;)

The other text was from an 'unknown caller'. Maybe Fabian had changed his number.

She opened it – it was from JASMINE.

Due to unforeseen circumstances we have brought forward our completion deadline to July 6th. We are anxious to finalise recruitment to the Institute as soon as possible. JASMINE Assignment Five therefore requires immediate attention. Your keywords are:
authority fake conceal reveal.
COMPLETED PORTFOLIOS SHOULD THEN BE HANDED TO YOUR SCHOOL MENTOR.
Late submissions not accepted.

Piggin' heck. What was JASMINE playing at? It meant she only had a week to complete it. She had wanted to do something big for assignment five. Make a splash, seal her place as a promising young journalist and convince the world to save itself before it was too late.

She got up and kicked the bed. Damn, damn, damn. She would have to think fast.

She paced the room, testing and rejecting ideas like she was speed-eating cherries and spitting out the stones. Eventually she had half a plan that could fit the **fake conceal reveal** part of the brief, but she would have to really reach to make **authority** fit too. But it would have to do: there wasn't time to mess about.

She returned to the computer and tapped impatiently into the search engine. There were rumours that some of the poverty protesters at the camp were not poor at all – and she had decided to dig the dirt on one of them. Maybe she could find something about the woman she had hit with the coke can. She typed eagerly then stopped. No – her

161

parents had warned her to leave that alone.

What about that other protester? The alpha male with the tan and the aftershave you could smell a mile off. What was the T-shirt he was wearing? She typed *'Kiss Me – I Can't Afford to Buy You Flowers'* into 'Images Search' and didn't have to look far before she found a picture of him posted on Snapzagram. There was a name to match the face: Daniel Bavington. He certainly sounded posh.

Ok. She had a target for her story.

Now it was up to her to get all the keywords to fit and make her final assignment as gripping as possible.

XL

Nobody gave her a second look as she strolled into the protest camp. She pulled the pom poms on her trapper hat so that it covered her face, and adjusted the plastic Harry Potter glasses she had bought in a fancy dress shop. Her grey pumps squeaked on the paving stones as she dodged between the tents searching for Daniel Bavington.

It was the weekend, so the camp was extra-crowded. A group of women was sitting in a circle listening to a monk reading poems. Jac sat amongst them; they smiled at her and somebody offered her a soggy-looking chickpea samosa. She pretended to eat it, then slipped it into her pocket.

Then she saw the gang of protesters who had thrown eggs at her on her way to school. They were sharing sushi outside a food tent, their pig masks discarded so they could enjoy their luxury meal. Daniel Bavington was among them, wearing a new T-shirt: *'POETRY NOT POVERTY'*. Jac watched him closely and when he broke away from the group she got up and followed him.

He walked about fifty metres, unzipped a bright blue tent and retrieved two bottles of wine from inside. Then he returned to his friends. Jac waited, then approached the tent. She opened the flap and got in, sealing the entrance.

Inside, a Gucci jacket was draped over an expensive coolbox. There was no sleeping bag; no overnight things. Bavington definitely went somewhere more comfortable at bedtime. Jac slipped her hands through the jacket pockets until she found a wallet. She looked over the contents: driving licence, credit cards. Within seconds she had Bavington's address. She used her phone to snap photos of the inside of the tent: champagne on ice inside the cool box, and a large hamper with a media system built into the lid, crammed full of luxury goodies.

There was a zipping noise behind her and the tent flap flew open. A leg entered the tent, white flesh bursting through a rip on a pair of designer jeans. Daniel Bavington was crouching down outside, ready to enter.

'Hey, Dan – get another glass! For Natasha!'

The leg didn't move. 'Is that Blonde Natasha?'

Jac held her breath. Daniel's leg disappeared again and he started talking to his friend – who was apparently called 'Bifter' – about whether Natasha was single.

Jac rummaged through the picnic hamper, her hands settling on a corkscrew. She plunged its sharp point into the base of the back of the tent and dragged it towards her, creating a long slit in the tent wall. She pulled herself through it, snatching her feet out of the way just as Daniel crawled back inside. Holding the torn fabric together, she listened as a clutch of wine glasses clinked together inside the tent.

A scuffing noise told her that Daniel was leaving.

She released the fabric and sat on her heels, waiting for Daniel and Bifter to leave. After a while she heard no sound, so she stood up and turned to walk away.

She found herself face to face with blue-eyed man dressed in denim, long blond dreadlocks cascading from a leather cap. He gripped her by the shoulder and brought his face so close to Jac's that, when he spoke, she could smell the sushi on his breath.

'Looks like I've caught a dirty rat,' he rasped. 'Do you know what we do to rats that sniff around our tents?'

Jac recognised his voice from earlier. 'You must be Bifter,' she said. 'I'm so glad I found you. I need to give you this.'

She dug into her pocket, took out the chickpea samosa and pushed it into his face. It was enough to make him let go of her for a moment, and she turned and ran. Then she heard him cry out in pain as the curry powder reacted with his eyes.

Her heart was pounding, and the splurge of adrenaline that shot through her made her want to laugh out loud. Not for the first time, she sprinted out of the protest camp to the sound of hateful shouting and insults.

Two streets away she walked into a charity shop and bought a pretty, floral top and a cute hairclip. She changed into her new clothes in the toilets of the burger bar next door. She took a taxi to Daniel Bavington's house, pressed the intercom buzzer on the gates and spoke to the housekeeper. She asked the cab driver to wait.

'Hi – I'm Bifter's kid sister. He's sent me round for Daniel's MP3 player? The old one?'

The housekeeper let her in. As she walked up the

drive, Jac took photos of Daniel's enormous, beautiful house. The housekeeper asked her to wait in the hallway, and as soon as she disappeared upstairs, Jac slipped into the surrounding rooms to take more photos: the drawing room, games room, home cinema and the biggest downstairs bathroom she had ever seen.

'There you go, my dear. I hope it's the right one.'

'I can always bring it back if it isn't. Thanks. Bye!'

She walked back up the drive, got in the cab, thanked the driver for waiting and asked him to take her home.

Her parents were in – and drunk.

'Darling!' Her mum's hair was messy on one side and flat on the other. 'That's such a pretty top! Isn't it, Julian?'

Her dad tried to focus on Jac before giving up and staring into his glass. 'Very nice,' he mumbled.

'You should *flare wowery* things more often! You look *nalmost ormal*.'

Jac eyed her mum and dad with interest. When she had searched Daniel's wallet in the tent, she had found her parents' business card. Which meant that Daniel was one of their clients. If she asked her parents the right questions, they could totally expose Daniel for the lying little rich boy he really was.

She felt for the stolen MP3 player in her pocket and pressed the 'record' button. Making sure that the device remained out of sight, she smiled sweetly at her parents ... and poured them two large drinks.

XLI

'Bank-note Bavington? He's a complete fraud,' said her dad. 'Went to public school, father's a big cheese in the City. Mother's a Bulgarian Duchess. Never done a day's work in his life.'

'All his anti-poverty nonsense is such a giggle, darling!' Her mum's mouth flopped into a squiffy smile. 'Last year we got him off a conviction for assaulting a tramp. Ha-ha! That's how much *he* cares about the poor.'

This was pure gold. Jac would make sure the truth about Bavington was splashed all over the papers. She would make him look like a nasty little goofhead.

'He's got fifty pound notes coming out of his spoilt little backside. We paid that magistrate a lot of money to get Daniel off. And he paid us double to do it.'

'It's all about getting rich, you see, darling,' said her mum. She waved her glass about like a flag.

'But you've helped him get away with being a liar,' said Jac.

'So what?' Her dad's face darkened. 'Where there's filth like him, there's money.' He swallowed the rest of his drink in a single gulp and frowned at her. 'Actually, Jacqueline, I think that top makes you look a bit of a tart.'

Jac's skin smarted in anger. Her mum waved her hands and looked at her as if to say 'don't upset him, you know what he's like'. But Jac turned away from her mum and fixed her eyes on her dad instead. 'Don't you care that you make all your money from supporting awful people with horrible beliefs?'

'I don't. And I don't care if I have to send you to bed for insolence, either.'

'Oh, Julian! Hush, now.' Her mum lurched towards the coffee table and poured him another glass of whisky. He tipped it down his throat; a mist came over his eyes and he flopped into the sofa. Not long afterwards, his eyes closed. Her mum watched him carefully, then spoke again.

'What you don't understand, Jaccy, is that we have to make money while we can,' she said. 'The truth is, that Britain is absolutely going to the dogs ... and we have to be ready.'

'For what?'

'God's Profiteers, darling! When they come, we have to hide.'

Did she just say 'God's Profiteers'? Jac's heart raced. Her mum's speech was slurred, and it sounded more like 'Gogz foffitiahs' – but ...

Her dad's eyelids dragged open to reveal a glare. 'Shut up, Flick. She doesn't need to know any of this yet.'

Her mum nodded and pretended to zip up her lips. 'Absolutely, darling. Right-o. Ssshh!'

The MP3 player in Jac's pocket let out a low beep, telling her that the batteries were low. She eyed her dad impatiently, waiting for his eyelids to droop again. Her mum watched him, too, and when he started breathing heavily she leant forward and spoke in a whisper.

'Don't worry, darling. When the Profiteers come, we'll be safe. We've been given a place at The Croft.'

Jac's heartbeat went up another notch on the scale: surely not the same place she read about when she was in the Home Secretary's office?

'Do you mean Glenoustie Croft?'

'Goodness – how do you know about that?' Her mum tried to stand up. 'Have they been asking you about your room?'

There was a grunt as her dad slumped deeper into the cushions. Her mum dragged herself upright and staggered to the living room door.

The MP3 beeped again and Jac willed it not to give up just yet.

'So there it is, darling. Mummy and Daddy have helped the government, and the government have agreed to help us back.' She steadied herself against the door frame. 'When Britain goes ... goes all wrong, we're going to escape from the poverty, and live in a lovely Glenoustie castle with lots of other important people. Won't that be nice?'

She blew Jac a kiss and almost fell out through the doorway.

Her dad snored disgustingly. Jac watched him for a few minutes, then slipped into his office and closed the door behind her. She switched on a small lamp, casting a pyramid of light onto the desk.

She searched through the filing cabinet. It didn't take long – her dad had labelled the God's Profiteers' file 'G.P.' There were letters inside, a very thick contract and three ID cards giving access to Glenoustie Croft: one for each of her parents, and one for her. She flicked through the pages of the contract.

It seemed to be some sort of deal between the Profiteers and the British government. On the final page, the Prime Minister and members of his cabinet had signed their names. There were also signatures for representatives of the Profiteers. Her parents' autographs were there, too. Jac switched on the scanner and slipped the contract onto the glass plate.

There was a crash and her dad stumbled up behind her. He grabbed her by the arm. Yanking her upwards, he drew her close to him and breathed a mixture of alcohol fumes and hatred into her face.

'How many times have I told you that this office is private?' He gave her a shove.

'This is research,' said Jac, daring to stare him out.

'In *my* filing cabinet?'

'For *my* portfolio. I'm applying for journalism college.'

A derogatory laugh spat out of his mouth. 'You?' he said. 'You'll never amount to anything. And you'll be a journalist over my dead body. They're the scum of the Earth.'

'I think you'll find that lawyers like you are the scum of the Earth,' said Jac. 'Bribing, manipulating, bending the law? It's disgusting what you do! You're supposed to be helping people who can't help themselves! But instead you make money out of dirty little liars like Daniel Bavington. At least journalists like me try to expose the truth!'

He let go of her and was silent – and, for a moment, Jac thought she had won the argument. But then he raised his hand and slapped her hard across the face. A vicious stinging crept across her skin and she felt an overwhelming urge to burst into tears. She steadied herself, refusing to cry.

'So – you're a fan of the truth?' he said coldly.

'Well get this, missy. We didn't want children. We didn't want you. Your mum tried to get rid of you but they didn't do it properly.'

Jac kept her eyes fixed on his, refusing to feel the pain.

'We sued, of course. We got big fat compensation for a lifetime of being stuck with you. And, in return, we've helped the hospital cover up every mistake they've made. Negligence, death. All brushed under the carpet, thanks to us.'

His mouth twitched into a smile. 'If you must be a pathetic little hack working in a grubby office somewhere, then go ahead. We couldn't be more disappointed in you than we are already.'

He stepped forward and removed the God's Profiteers contract from the scanner.

'And don't you ever poke your snotty little nose into my business again. Go to your room and make sure I don't have to look at you tomorrow morning.'

'No problem,' said Jac.

Inside her pocket, she switched off the MP3 player. She looked her dad straight in the eye, then turned and walked away.

XLII

Jac closed her bedroom door behind her. Her dad's cruel words had got into her blood and turned it cold.

She made a copy of the recording of her parents and saved it to her computer. She printed off photographs of Daniel Bavington's house and the inside of his tent. She grabbed a notepad and pen and hastily wrote a letter. When she had finished, she put the letter and photos in a large envelope with Daniel's MP3 player. She pulled on a baggy cardigan, strode into the hall, opened the front door and went out into the night.

The cool air soothed her, and she walked quickly. But when she arrived at the protest camp, her heart sank. It looked completely different in the dark, and she could only guess where Daniel's tent might be. She stood at the edge, staring at the hotchpotch of semi-circular silhouettes stretching out into the gloom.

'Hello again.' It was the monk who had been reading poetry earlier. 'You look a bit lost.'

'I am,' said Jac. 'Dan Bavington said I could use his tent tonight, but I can't work out where I'm going.'

'I'm sure I can help.'

The monk wove his way through the tents, his sandals barely making a sound as he moved.

'I've been here since the beginning,' he said. 'I've watched tents go up and tents come down. I've met folk from every part of the world; I feel as if I've made a million friends.'

He took her hand and guided her through a tightly packed group of tents. 'I think this is the one you are looking for.'

Jac squinted at it uncertainly.

'Can I get you something to eat? A samosa? You look tired.'

'No – but thank you.'

The monk pressed his hands together, bowed his head and padded off into the dark.

The zip on Daniel's tent buzzed noisily as Jac pulled it open and climbed inside. She sat cross-legged on the floor, pulled her phone out of her pocket and, by the light of the menu screen, re-read her note:

'YOU ARE A FRAUD.
THE DAY AFTER TOMORROW,
I WILL SEND THESE PHOTOS AND AN
EDITED VERSION OF THIS MP3 RECORDING
TO THE PRESS.
THE TRUTH ABOUT YOU WILL BE
SPLATTERED OVER EVERY
NEWSPAPER.
YOU WILL BE A COMPLETE JOKE.
BUT YOU CAN STOP IT.
YOUR LAWYERS ARE **CORRUPT**. EXPOSE
THEM.
PUBLISH THE FULL MP3 RECORDING AND

LET THE WORLD KNOW WHAT THE
STRYDER-JONESES ARE REALLY LIKE.

DO IT BY 6 PM TOMORROW EVENING AND
YOUR PATHETIC STORY WILL BE SAFE.
SO – RICH BOY,
IT'S EITHER YOU ... OR THEM.'

She sealed the envelope and addressed it to 'D. BAVINGTON, POSH TWIT AND LIAR.'

She propped the envelope up against a bottle of champagne.

At last, she had a dynamic story to complete her portfolio. What had started out as a dull exposé of a bored little rich boy had turned into a betrayal of the highest order. None of the other students would have tackled the brief in the way she had. JASMINE would be stunned by her originality and guts.

Could any of the other applicants have been reckless enough to defy the ultimate **authority** in any teenager's life?

She had betrayed her parents with a story that would send them to prison.

As she zipped the tent shut, she didn't care if she ever saw her mum and dad again.

XLIII

Two days later, when Jac got up, she could hear her mum clattering about in the kitchen. So – they hadn't been arrested just yet.

Her dad was in the bathroom, so she walked along the hallway and stuck her head round the kitchen door. Her mum was trying to open a packet of pain-au-chocolat and her tongue stuck out of the corner of her mouth as she fiddled with the wrapping.

'Here, let me,' said Jac.

'That's very sweet, darling. Thank you.'

Jac ripped the packaging apart and the pastries tumbled out onto a plate. She and her mum helped themselves at the same time, both of them biting into the bottom right hand corner and patting crumbs away from their lips as they ate.

'Yummy, aren't they, darling?'

Jac nodded – then surprised herself by leaning forward and planting a kiss on her mum's cheek. Her mum stopped chewing for a moment, and touched her cheek where the kiss had been.

'Goodbye, mum,' said Jac.

Her mum took another bite. 'Goodness, darling,' she said, spraying out crumbs. 'You sound as if you won't be coming back.'

'Oh – *I'll* be back,' said Jac. She was already halfway out the door.

'Seeya, dad!' She shouted as she passed the bathroom, to make sure he heard her. She packed her school things and left.

At the tube station she went straight to the news kiosk and bought a paper. Daniel Bavington's picture was on the front page. She stood on the escalator and read the article underneath.

THAT'S RICH COMING FROM HIM!
THE POVERTY PROTESTER
WHO IS LIVING A LIE

That wasn't what it was supposed to say. Where were the shocking revelations about the famous Stryder-Joneses, their disgusting cover-ups, and their dubious connection with the British government? Desperately, she searched through the rest of the paper.

The bottom of the escalator nearly tripped her up. She got on the next train, and tore through the paper again, discarding unwanted sheets on the floor and drawing loud tuts from the other passengers.

There was nothing in the paper about her parents or the government at all. Nothing. What the piggin' heck had Bavington done? Why had he turned himself in instead of them? It didn't make sense.

She left the carriage, and walked to school in a foul mood, vowing to go straight to the library and read every single newspaper before registration. Somebody *must* have picked up the story about her mum and dad.

Fabian and Freddy were inside the school

entrance, handing out flyers for their drama club production. Freddy saw her and came over.

'You looked stressed,' he said.

Jac sighed and took one of the drama club leaflets. 'I'm looking forward to this, though.'

'Ah.' Freddy's eyes widened and he looked over his shoulder at Fabian. 'He doesn't want you to come.'

The flyer crumpled between Jac's fingers. 'That's ok. I'm ... cool with that.   So ... have you two made up, then?' she said.

'Yes. But it's early days.'

'I'm glad.'

'I should get back ...'

'Sure. Did you tell him what I said?'

'Yes.'

Jac looked towards Fabian and bit her lip. 'Will you tell him again, please?'

'Of course. Look – there'll be a DVD of the show. Perhaps you could ...'

'Thanks.'

Freddy walked back to Fabian and Jac took the stairs to the second floor.

Another student was in the library looking at the papers. Jac knew from his indifferent reaction to her, that nothing about her parents had been published. She spent the rest of day in a daze, staring out of windows, doodling in margins and picking at the zip on her pencil case.

When she got home her mum had left her a note.

Darling,

Daddy and I have decided to go on a little holiday.

177

I'm sure you won't mind – Daddy thinks you'll be fine on your own. Delivery from Fortnum's arriving at 6pm – some nice treats for you.
If you need anything, call Francesca.
Mummy

That was weird – but she was glad to have the place to herself. She only had forty-eight hours to write up her assignment, and it was going to take a huge effort to make her story about the secret life of Daniel Bavington sound impressive. Her head was spinning with questions about why such a selfish pig would sacrifice his own reputation and save two corrupt lawyers from prison.

She switched on the computer.

With quivering fingers, she prepared to type the final words of her JASMINE portfolio.

XLIV

Miss Steele's eyes flashed with interest behind the glass wall of her spectacles, her cherry pink lips pursed into a half smile. Jac's completed portfolio, freshly printed on spotless white paper, lay in her hands.

'You broke into a hospital?' she said. 'Wow. JASMINE loves that kind of thing.'

Jac allowed herself to feel a surge of pride and relaxed into her chair. She recounted her article in her head, waiting with relish for the paragraph that revealed that she had – no less – located and spoken to Richard Masters. Miss Steele was going to be *really* impressed when she read that.

The revelation was due at the top of the next page. Jac was sure nobody else would have interviewed the ex-Prime Minister. Miss Steele turned the paper over with a flick of her finger.

Within seconds, a dark cloud disfigured her face. Her sapphire eyes cooled. Her lips contracted into a tight, unforgiving band of muscle. The colour of her skin shifted to grey.

'What the hell is this?' she drawled. Even her voice sounded different.

'I thought ...'

'Don't think. Don't ever think again.' Miss Steele skim-read the rest of the portfolio, her expression becoming more hateful with every turn of the page. She pulled Jac's memory stick from the computer and dropped it on the floor.

'So it was you who organised that ridiculous flash mob. I knew we should have tried harder to stop it!' With a single jab of her black, shiny stiletto heel, Miss Steele crushed the memory stick into splinters.

'What are you doing, you mad cow?' Jac lunged forward and tried to grab the paper copy.

Miss Steele raised the document out of Jac's reach. With her other hand, she seized Jac's throat and pinned her up against the wall. Jac gasped in panic.

'You stupid girl.' Miss Steele threw the portfolio across the room and a hundred sheets of typed white paper cascaded to the ground. She took out her telephone and, applying more pressure to Jac's neck, dialled a number. Somebody answered quickly.

'There's a problem,' said Miss Steele. 'We have an insubordinate. Activate Operation Rat-Trap. You have my location. Send a collection team now.'

Jac tried to kick Miss Steele's shins. Miss Steele slipped her phone into her pocket and punched Jac swiftly in the stomach. A cry of pain rose in Jac's throat but was suppressed by Miss Steele's gripped fingers.

'What's going on?' Jac forced her voice to seep out of her constricted windpipe with a croak. 'You said I could be a good journalist ...'

'Shut up, you little freak.' Miss Steele's hand squeezed harder. 'There is no journalism college.' Her skinny lips sneered. 'JASMINE doesn't want journalists. It wants kids who hate authority. Selfish little daredevils who will stop at nothing to get attention. It wants screwed-up little rebels like you. It wants an army of heartless, teenage soldiers to destroy this stupid country and bring it, snivelling, to its knees.'

Not enough blood was circulating into Jac's head. She felt dizzy and sick.

'Nobody was going to train you to be a star reporter. Nobody cares how good you are at writing. JASMINE is an international agency for child terrorists. You were supposed to be one.' Miss Steele increased the pressure; a grey veil clouded Jac's vision and her ears started ringing.

'You weren't supposed to have a freaking conscience, and you weren't supposed to find out the truth. We should have had Masters killed ages ago. Now he will be. And you ...' The bony hand clamped harder still. 'You will go missing on the way home from school tonight and your body will never be found.'

The grey turned to black; the buzzing in Jac's ears became a heavenly peal of bells. Pins and needles fizzed from her fingertips, along her arms and into her chest. Miss Steele's voice morphed into a slow motion, indistinct drone. Her perfume smelt like death.

Jac thought of Fabian, and Freddy's hypnotic eyes. She thought about Gary ... and Colette.

Her muscles slowly melted and her body slid to the floor.

XLV

A girl called Bryony Mendelsohn was standing in the English lab looking at Jac.

'I left my pencil case,' she seemed to be saying.

Miss Steele had stepped away and was glaring at a kooky, floral pouch on a table at the back of the class. 'Sure. Go get it,' she said.

'Is she OK?' said Bryony.

'Just a little light-headed,' said Miss Steele. 'You girls never eat enough.'

Bryony wandered off towards the rear of the lab. Miss Steele watched her impatiently.

Jac tried to get to her feet, but Miss Steele lunged forward and, with Bryony's back turned, went again for Jac's throat. But Jac was ready for her and bit hard into Miss Steele's hand. Miss Steele let out a yelp, and Bryony turned round and gawped.

'Hey, Bryony,' said Jac. 'Give us a hand and walk with me to the medical room, yeah?'

'That won't be necessary,' snapped Miss Steele.

But Bryony was a sweet girl, and once the idea of helping Jac was planted in her head, she could not be persuaded otherwise.

'Thanks, Bry – you're a real pal.'

'Awww!' said Bryony, and the two of them

walked out of the lab.

The door closed behind them. Miss Steele watched Jac through the glass and took out her phone.

*

Jac stared out of the medical room window at the street below. She touched her collar to make sure it was turned up and hiding the marks on her neck. The school nurse looked over briefly and went back to her paperwork. Out in the street, a van pulled up and parked close to the school gates. There were two men sitting in the front, darkly dressed and taking turns to watch the building.

A few Year Twelve students spilled out onto the pavement, taking advantage of a free period. The van window on the driver's side slid down and the men watched the gate more intently. With a shiver, Jac guessed that the men had been sent by JASMINE to dispose of her.

Her stomach writhed and she asked the nurse for a drink of water. Why? Why did JASMINE want to use child terrorists to ruin the country? Why had they tried to sabotage her flash mob? Why did they hate the truth so much? None of it made any sense.

The cold water hit the pit of her stomach. A jumbled montage of images swooped through her head: Miss Steele's cold eyes, her hand around her neck; the revelation that JASMINE was a lie; the shadowy figures outside, waiting to take her away in the van and murder her. The images circled in a sickening kaleidoscope. Then came the chilling realisation that she was SO selfish and horrible, that JASMINE wanted her to be a terrorist. With a wretched moan, Jac bent double and vomited on the floor.

The nurse hurried over and helped Jac to the couch. She slipped a pillow under her head, and tucked a blanket around Jac's shivering body. Jac half-watched the nurse clean up the vomit and tried not to breathe in the smell of disinfectant as it wafted across the room.

'Sorry,' she murmured later, as the nurse returned the mop and bucket to the cupboard.

The nurse smiled sympathetically. 'You really should try and get some fluid inside you,' she said.

'Got any Lucozade?' Jac pulled herself up onto one elbow.

The nurse poured her a glass.

'Thanks.'

Jac sipped slowly, and this time the drink stayed down. The glucose and caffeine gave her the lift she needed, and she began to think about how she could get home without JASMINE finding her. She walked over to the window: the van was still there. The nurse took her temperature and found it to be normal; Jac persuaded her that she was over-tired and that she'd be fine if she went home early and got some sleep. The nurse signed her off school and Jac picked up her bag and went.

It was afternoon recess, which meant that the corridors were busy with students. Even if Miss Steele was waiting somewhere for her, it would be impossible for her to take Jac away without being noticed. She made her way to the library and looked out over the rear entrance. A car with blacked-out windows was waiting on the opposite side of the street. As she watched, a figure in a baseball cap got out and crossed the road. He raised a finger to one ear and seemed to be talking into some sort of hands-free device. He positioned himself by the rear gate and waited.

The west entrance was also being watched. Jac fired off a text.

Get ur screwed-up butt over here now. Library. URGENT!!!!!!!

A reply came back instantly.

What's in it for me?

Jac swallowed hard.

Not finding out tomorrow that I'm dead.

Freddy appeared in the library soon after.

'Have you got one of those ... key thingies on you?' asked Jac.

'Never leave home without one,' said Freddy.

'Can I borrow it?'

He looked at her thoughtfully. 'Something serious is going on, isn't it?'

'Don't ask questions,' said Jac.

Freddy nodded. He rummaged in a pocket and passed the lock pick under the table. Jac pushed it down her sock.

'Did you tell Fabes what I said?' she asked.

Freddy had no return message to pass on.

'Please tell him again. Loudly.' She heard her voice crack. 'And – look after him.'

Freddy frowned, but said nothing and headed back to class.

The corridors were empty now and Jac made her way nervously to the old science block. She used Freddy's lock-picking tool to break into a lab that was being refurbished. She pushed her way through the dustsheets and went out through a fire door. To the right was another laboratory, and there was a narrow gap between the lab wall and the perimeter of the school. Jac squeezed along it, disturbing a couple of Year Elevens who were sharing a cigarette in a pungent cloud of tobacco smoke.

'I won't tell if you don't,' she said, pressing past them.

At the other end were the remains of an old vegetable garden, now overgrown with brambles. A tatty old gate was barely visible in the corner. The briars lashed at her clothes and snagged her skin; she bit her lip in pain as she forced her way to the gate. She worked the strange-shaped tool into the lock, twisting it until she felt a click. With an aching creak, the gate opened. The back street on the other side was empty. Jac closed the gate and ran away.

She hailed a taxi on the main road and asked the driver to take her home. He dropped her off at the end of her street. As she neared the front door, the side of a people carrier slid open, and a man and a woman strode towards her.

She turned and ran. The buzz from the Lucozade had gone and her legs felt sluggish, like they did in her nightmares. A hand grabbed her sleeve – she swung her schoolbag hard and caught the man in the face. He let go, blood pouring into his right eye: Jac's Screaming Puppies zip fob had torn his eyelid. The woman paused to look, and it was enough for Jac to get a few strides' advantage. She fled up the street, the woman's footsteps pounding again behind her.

There was a pedestrian crossing ahead, the green man flashing and warning her to stop. The woman's breath would be warm on the back of her neck at any minute. Now the red man shone, like a human-shaped blood splat above her. Jac stopped. Rush hour traffic sped over the crossing in both directions.

Her heart bursting through her chest, she knew

she was seconds away from when the woman's hand would snatch her and take her to her death. With a twitch of her legs, Jac darted into the busy road.

Halfway across, she hesitated. Five sharp fingernails dug into her arm and yanked her backwards, and a voice spat in her ear:

'Got you.'

XLVI

Jac pulled away across the road, dragging the woman behind her.

As she leapt onto the opposite kerb, there was a scream of tyres and a sickening bang. A white van struck the woman and she was catapulted away from Jac, bouncing up the windscreen and over the roof like a rag doll. Then her body dropped onto the tarmac. There was a brief silence, then screaming. People rushed to help. The van did not stop, disappearing in a cloud of dark fumes. Jac put her head down and walked round the corner without looking back.

She got on the first bus that came by, watching for signs that she was being followed. For nearly two hours, she swapped buses many times, not knowing where she was or where she was going. A tiny old lady sat next to her, told her she looked pale and gave her a five pound note and a toffee. Jac chewed hungrily, and tried not to cry at such kindness.

Finally she relaxed. The street signs told her she was in NW10, an area of London she didn't know. She got off the bus, and spent the old lady's five pounds in a tea shop, watching the door as she hungrily ate a club sandwich. She used her mum's credit card to draw some cash at the till, and bought a couple of pastries and a bottle of water.

She walked aimlessly, wondering where she would sleep that night. There was no way she could go home. Then she saw a triple stone arch embellished with carvings and columns. A sign told her that this was Kensal Green Cemetery and that closing time was five o'clock. Jac looked at her watch: it was five to. One of the gates in the central arch was already shut, and she slipped inside.

Immediately the noise from the traffic subsided and the leafy pathways calmed her. The gravestones stood like giant dominoes, blackened over time by Victorian smoke and smudged with lichen. Behind her, a metallic creak told her that the gate was being locked.

Further in, neglected memorial stones drooped at forlorn angles, the words on them obscured by clumps of grass. Then there were trees, and a canal beyond. An abandoned mausoleum had partially collapsed, creating a nook where one wall had fallen against another. It was damp inside, but there was enough space for her to lie down.

She sat outside this makeshift den. With nothing else to do, she opened her school bag and did her homework. Then she ate one of the pastries, chewing it slowly and making it last half an hour.

When the sugar rush wore off, a deep tiredness crept over her. She crawled into the gap between the ancient stone slabs and fell asleep with the sun still bright in the sky.

She awoke at half past one in the morning. The moisture from the ground had seeped into her clothes and they were soaking. She crawled out and stood up, tugging her shirt away from her skin in disgust. The moon was half full, and cast a luminosity over the gravestones, creating ghoulish shapes and shadows, dark recesses and black unknowns.

A fox screamed nearby and made her jump. A fallen angelic statue lay horizontal in thick undergrowth, one hand spookily outstretched towards the stars. The horrible image of the woman from JASMINE flailing over the back of the van returned to haunt Jac. It was as if the woman's corpse was right there in front of her in the dark.

Only daylight would banish these thoughts. Jac found a pac-a-mac at the bottom of her schoolbag, wondering why she hadn't remembered it before. She spread it on the ground, sat with her back to the mausoleum, hugged her knees and waited for morning.

XLVII

After three nights in the cemetery Jac was beginning to feel unwell. Scabby sores had appeared on her hips and shoulders from lying on the damp ground and – from the way that the other customers were looking at her as she ate her breakfast in the café – she knew that she smelt bad. She finished her hot chocolate and ran to the mini supermarket opposite.

She filled her basket with scented soap, a flannel, handwash for clothes and a four-litre bottle of water. She found a pair of children's white socks that looked big enough to fit, and some antiseptic cream for the scabs. They even sold disposable paper knickers. She hoiked everything onto the counter and handed the shop assistant her mum's credit card.

A red light flashed on the card swiper.

'I am very sorry, my dear, but your card has been refused.' The shop assistant smiled apologetically. 'Do you have another you can try?'

Jac shook her head and rummaged in her purse for cash. She had just enough to buy the water, flannel and knickers. The shopkeeper glanced at her grubby clothes as he opened up the till.

You have a pound change, my dear,' he said.

'No ...' began Jac. She was sure she'd added it up

right.

'Definitely one pound change,' said the shopkeeper. He had kind eyes. 'You take care now.'

Jac walked out, and a few minutes later noticed that the man had slipped the little bar of soap into the carrier bag with the rest of the shopping.

She returned to the cemetery. A door in the archway opened and a man with a little toothbrush moustache ran out and told her to stop. He was holding her school bag – and the sleeping bag she had bought from a camping shop two days ago.

'I've phoned your school,' he said. 'Gave 'em a description. Turns out they've been wondering where you are.'

Jac made a dart for the street, but the caretaker lunged forward and grabbed her.

'And I've rung social services, just like the school said.' He was enjoying feeling important. 'They're on their way. You 'ave to wait here until they arrive.' He marched her into an old-fashioned office. He took her shopping and told her to sit down.

'No doubt these are stolen,' he said, poking around in the bag. He pulled out the packet of knickers and dropped them, his face squirming in embarrassment. Jac raised his eyebrows at him and smirked.

'Well, anyway. You're not keeping 'em,' he muttered, scuttling out of the room.

The moment the key turned in the lock, Jac got up, climbed out of the small window at the back of the office, ran across the grass and pulled herself over the railings into the street. That was easy – she'd clocked the open window as soon as she'd walked in.

She jumped on a bus, and swapped routes randomly, just as she had done on the day she'd fled from school. She allowed the buses to take her further and further out of London, hoping that JASMINE, the social services – and probably the police – would be concentrating their search in the centre of the city. Then she thought she saw the bus driver eyeing her suspiciously whilst talking into his radio, and decided that the buses were not safe after all.

She got off and walked. There was a church coffee shop on the corner, and Jac went inside and spent her last pound on a cup of tea and a biscuit. It did not nourish her, and later, when the smell from a fish and chip shop made her salivate and her stomach moan, she slipped round the back of the shops and rummaged through the dustbins. She found an unopened plastic bag containing four soft white rolls that were past their 'best before' date, ripped open the packaging and chewed hungrily. Then, dizzy from the sudden injection of carbohydrate, she staggered behind the bins and fell asleep.

When she awoke it was dark. A couple of metres away, a tramp was urinating against the shop wall. A group of kids walked by, half-drunk on a bottle of cider, and when they saw the tramp they started pushing him. The tramp made a swipe at them; it took him off balance and he fell over. The teenagers laughed and ran off. Jac hid behind the bin until their drunken laughter had faded to nothing.

She was still holding a half-eaten roll. She approached the tramp and, seeing that he was getting up, smiled and offered him the bread.

'Bugger off.' The tramp rose above her, blasting vomit-smelling breath into her face.

'I'm not ...'

'If I see you again I'll punch yer brains out!'

She fled round the corner. A police car crawled by and she turned her face away from the glare of its headlamps. A woman passed her, and Jac asked her directions to the nearest tube station. The woman looked at her with fear and disgust, and hurried away.

Music throbbed from a car as it drove past, and someone threw a kebab wrapped in newspaper out of the car window. The kebab bounced into the gutter, and the draught from the car blew the newspaper across the street. A double sheet wrapped itself around Jac's ankles, greasy and smudged. As she removed it, she saw the writing:

'The former Prime Minister Richard Masters was transferred to an undisclosed high security facility by private ambulance yesterday, after being assessed by a team of experts who arrived, unannounced, at the Stockbridge Mental Health Institute. Manager Liz Malhotra expressed surprise at the visit, saying 'Mr Masters has shown an improvement of late, and we were confident of a full recovery. But I have complete faith in the team who visited us. We wish Richard all the best.'

Jac's guts clenched with sorrow.

JASMINE had done what they said they would do. They had duped the staff at Stockbridge, taken Masters away and murdered him. She slumped against a lamppost and buried her face in her hands.

She couldn't do this on her own any more. Without Masters to lead the country, the situation was desperate. It was time to swallow her pride – and risk the biggest rejection of her life.

There wasn't anyone else. She was going to have to visit Fabian and ask him to help her.

XLVIII

Jac headed for central London, the tube carriage clanking along the tracks. She watched the lights blur against the dark walls of the tunnels, punctuated every few minutes by a gaudy mass of faces that spilled towards her when the doors opened.

She changed trains twice, always checking behind her, finally getting out at Hampstead station and taking a meandering route to the leafy street where Fabian lived with his family. She stopped behind a tree and looked towards Fabian's house. On the opposite side of the road, a pinprick of golden-red light moved up and down as somebody smoked a cigarette. Then a car door opened and the light from inside illuminated the smoker as they climbed in. They looked wrong: dark parka and trousers, hood up. There were three more people hunched inside the car. It was enough to convince Jac that Fabian's house was being watched.

She hurried back the way she had come. When she reached the house on the corner, she climbed the garden wall and dropped into the shrubbery the other side. She and Fabian had been sneaking through this garden since they were at prep school, and the owners had never noticed. There was a shed at the far end; Jac climbed onto the roof, rolled over the top and dropped down into Fabian's garden, which was the other side. She crossed the lawn and climbed a fire escape to the roof terrace. She wrapped her arms round the cowl on the top of the nearest chimney and dragged it off. Then she lowered herself into the chimney. It was a few years since she had done this, and it was a tight squeeze.

Notches had been cut in the bricks more than a century ago, so that children sent to sweep the chimney had something to hold on to. Jac climbed downwards, blinking away dust and soot. Fabian's bedroom was at the top of the house and, as she dropped the last metre into the grate, Jac squealed and landed with a thump in an inky-grey cloud of dirt.

At first she thought Fabian wasn't there. She rubbed the grime out of her eyes and then she saw them: Fabian and Freddy, spooned together on the bed, eyes closed, two sets of headphones plugged into a single MP3 player. Fabian's arms were looped around Freddy's torso, and his fingers gently tapped out the beat of the music on Freddy's wrist.

A pang of jealousy punched Jac in the stomach. She had never seen two people look so comfortable together. She watched them awkwardly for a while, chewing the side of her thumbnail. Finally she picked up one of Fabian's scarves, rolled it into a loose ball and threw it at the bed.

It mostly hit Freddy, who opened his eyes slowly. He didn't react at first, then swore at the sight of an intruder. Then he recognised Jac and his eyebrows quivered in amusement.

'What the flippin' heck do you look like?' he grinned.

Fabian sat up, wondering why his earphones had come out of his ears. He saw Jac, glowered and looked away in disgust.

'I'm in trouble,' said Jac.

'We can see that,' said Freddy.

'I need your help.'

'You need a bath!' said Freddy.

Jac looked at the muck she had brought with her from the chimney. 'Sorry – I had to come that way ... I'm being followed.'

'Yeah, right ...' Fabian flicked a loose thread on the duvet.

'I am! And your house is being watched.'

Fabian shook his head, but Freddy got up and went out along the landing. After a few moments he returned.

'She's right,' said Freddy. 'There's a car opposite.'

'D'you know who it is?' Fabian's voice trembled.

'JASMINE,' said Jac.

'Oh, it piggin' well would be.' Fabian sucked his teeth in contempt and turned his back on her completely.

Freddy shrugged at Jac, as if to say 'Keep talking. He'll come round in the end.'

Where was she supposed to start? Tell them that JASMINE was a guerrilla organisation plotting to destroy Britain? That they had been grooming her to become a terrorist? That Miss Steele had tried to kill her? It sounded ridiculous. So she began with the moment she handed her completed assignment to Miss Steele. The muscles on the back of Fabian's neck tightened, and he didn't turn round.

But Freddy was listening, his eyelids occasionally blinking as he reclined on the bed. When Jac had finished, Fabian dropped his head into his hands.

'Oh God,' he groaned. 'Miss Steele kept asking me where you were.' His fingers muffled his voice. 'Funnily enough she didn't mention she wanted you dead.'

'What did you tell her?'

'Fortunately for you, I told her I didn't know and I didn't care.'

'Thanks a bunch,' smiled Jac.

'You're welcome.' He turned and looked at her at last. There was pain in his eyes – and it was Jac's turn to look away.

'The question is,' said Freddy, 'what do we do now?'

Downstairs, somebody hammered on the front door. Fabian's mum walked along the hall and spoke through the intercom system. As she talked, words like 'sorry' and 'no thank you' filtered up the stairs, her Jamaican accent sounding gentle and melodious.

Then there was a loud crack and a series of heavy thuds – and Fabian's mum screamed from the bottom of the stairs.

'Someone's trying to get in!' Fabian dug his fingers into his hair. He moved swiftly about the room, stuffing clothes, snacks and his wallet into a sports bag. He dug out a sweater and gave it to Jac.

'Get your shoes on, Fred,' he said.

Fabian's mum fled up the stairs, shouting to Fabian to lock his bedroom door and stay inside.

'I've pressed the emergency button, darling!' she yelled. 'MI5 are on their way!'

Jonas ran out onto the first floor landing, crying.

'It's all right, baby, Mummy's here!'

Down below, there was a bang as the front door split open and shards of wood catapulted along the hallway. Jonas's bedroom door slammed shut and Fabian's mum locked herself in, Jonas's cries now muffled inside.

Fabian strode to the fireplace. 'Come on,' he said. 'Chimney.'

People were running around on the ground floor. Fabian helped Jac climb into the grate. Freddy joined them, his eyes ablaze.

'Are we about to go on the run?' he said.

Footsteps pounded up the stairs. In the street, there was a screech of brakes and an amplified, metallic voice boomed a warning into the hallway. The protection squad had arrived outside.

Fabian gave Jac a leg up the chimney, and she scrambled upwards. She heard Freddy following close behind her. The intruders had reached both landings and were trying all the doors. Fabian's voice spiralled up into the sooty cavity as he too began to climb.

'Going on the run?' he said. 'You piggin' bet we are.'

XLIX

Sirens wailed in the distance behind them. Jac burst on to the Finchley Road with Freddy and Fabian close behind her. They ran across four lanes of traffic, car horns hooting angrily.

They dodged down the nearest side road, slowing their pace to a brisk walk, air plunging into their lungs as they tried to get their breath back.

'What are we going to do? We can't go on public transport looking this filthy,' said Fabian, spitting on his hands and wiping them on the inside of his jacket.

Freddy dipped down to check himself in the wing mirror of a parked car.

'Lordy love a duck! I look like a complete fright!'

'We all do,' said Jac.

'Here.' Fabian grabbed a T-shirt from his bag. They took turns to wipe the soot from their faces, rubbing the cotton cloth hard into their skin.

Freddy walked ahead and peered down a turn-off to the right. 'This way,' he called.

There was a minicab office halfway down. Heavy music thumped from an open door and the words *Colin's Cab and Courier Co.* flickered on and off in red neon.

'Perfect,' said Freddy. 'No questions asked here.'

A flight of stairs led upwards into the gloom. At the top was a tiny room with peeling wallpaper and a pile of dirty newspapers on a table.

'A cab to Stevenage Place, please. At the back of Oxford Street,' said Freddy.

They were told to wait, and sat on pockmarked chairs next to a sleeping drunk. The receptionist watched them from his reinforced glass booth, slowly chewing through a bag of enormous, oily chips.

Several people came and went, collecting parcels and dodgy-looking envelopes that Jac was sure were full of cash. A driver finally turned up, took one look at the drunk, and gestured that the teenagers follow him back onto the street. His car had a crack in the windscreen, and when they piled inside, two of the seatbelts didn't work and the driver glared at them in the rear view mirror.

'Hold the belts round you so they look OK,' he said.

Fabian and Freddy pulled the belts across their chests and the cab lunged forwards.

The driver took them through the back streets, a thick cigarillo hanging out of his mouth and belching smoke into the car. It seemed to take forever to reach central London. When they arrived at Stevenage Place the driver stuck out his sausage-fingers to take the money Fabian had pulled out of his wallet.

'No – wait,' said Freddy. He peered at the junction ahead of them. It was the street that led to his basement den. 'Stay here a mo,' he said, and he slipped out of the taxi door.

'Where's he gone?' snapped the driver. 'Sixteen pounds fifty! You pay me now!' His hand shot inside his jacket and he pulled out a knife. A thick blade flashed as he lunged over the back of the seat, slashing the air in front of Fabian's face. Fabian shrank back. He took a twenty-pound note from his wallet and handed it over.

'Keep the change, ducky.'

The driver harrumphed and put the knife away.

Outside, Freddy reached the end of the narrow road and stopped. With a jump he turned and ran back to the car.

'Police!' he said. 'They're raiding my place.'

At the word 'police', the cab driver stamped on the accelerator and the cab pulled away, tyres screeching like banshees on the tarmac. Freddy was only half inside the car and was thrown backwards, one leg dangling out of the open door. Fabian grabbed him with both hands, but there was no seat belt to hold him and he, too, was flung towards the door as the car swerved violently to the right. Jac grabbed hold of Fabian and steadied him.

'Slow down, you piggin' lunatic!' she shouted.

But the driver wasn't stopping.

Jac twisted in her seatbelt and hooked a leg through Fabian's. Anchored, Fabian managed to get both his arms around Freddy's torso, and tugged him inwards. Freddy scrambled into a sitting position, pulling his leg inside. Within a second, the car door was hit by a bollard on the pavement and slammed shut with a crunch.

They drove on, the car swerving like a rollercoaster.

Eventually the cab slowed, and the driver's face became less purple. Finally he pulled over and opened a can of beer to calm his nerves.

'I think it's time to get out,' said Jac.

'How much?' said Fabian to the driver.

'Twenty more.'

'I think someone's taking the mickey,' said Fabian. He handed the money over.

The whoop of a siren bounced off the surrounding buildings. A police motorcycle pulled out of a side street and blocked the cab's path. The cab driver swore under his breath. The police officer approached and told everyone to get out of the car. The officer asked to see the driver's documents and initiated a breathalyser test.

'You kids all right? Just wait there a minute, please.'

The cabbie was surprisingly quiet. He handed over some papers and the policeman radioed the details. The voice at the other end leaked out of the radio in fits and starts, metallic and indistinct. After a while the officer seemed to look less at the cab driver and his documents – and more at Jac and the boys. The voice on the radio talked at length; the cab driver was near enough to hear what was being said and he also turned and looked at the teenagers with interest.

Jac's heart revved up behind her ribs: she was sure the radio operator was giving a description of her, Freddy and Fabian in turn. The words *'trespass'*, *'truancy'*, *'shoplifting'* and *'social services'* seemed to filter from the radio receiver into the night air.

'Roger that.' The policeman stepped towards them.

'Can you tell me your names and addresses, please?' he said. He told the operator to 'stand by'.

'I'll go first,' said Freddy. He bowed flamboyantly. 'My name is Samson Hinks.'

'And I'm Elvis Donker,' said Fabian.

'Mindy Sensicle,' said Jac.

'*And we all live in a windmill in old Amsterdam,*' sang Fabian.

There was a bang as the taxi door slammed shut. The cabbie had run to his car and he drove off, the cab smashing into the police motorbike. The bike skidded across the road in a shower of sparks, and the cab disappeared in a belch of burning rubber. The policeman ran to inspect the damage, radioing for assistance.

'Run!' said Freddy.

They sprinted off the main road and into a shopping precinct. The sound of booted footsteps behind them meant that the policeman had given chase. They ran hard and turned right. Fabian grabbed Jac and they dived into a shop doorway. Freddy crouched behind a litter bin opposite; he signalled to Fabian and they both got ready. The policeman ran round the corner; Fabian and Freddy jerked their arms and the officer's feet flew from underneath him. He fell heavily, twisting his ankle and landing on his face. Fabian and Freddy stood up, leaving Fabian's scarf entangled in the officer's ankles.

There was a squeal of brakes. A squad car careened into the precinct behind them. Two female officers got out: one attended their injured colleague and the other, fresh and fast, took up the chase.

'Nearly there,' shouted Freddie, racing ahead.

They all ran into a narrow Victorian street with grim-looking brick buildings on either side. Only a few metres behind, the officer shouted at them to stop. Freddy turned left, and Jac and Fabian followed him past a creepy old workhouse and into a side street.

204

Freddy was hunched in an archway, picking the lock of a heavy, blue metal door. The padlock clicked and he heaved the door open. They rushed inside, the three of them grasping the metal and pulling it to. As it clanked shut, the policewoman came round the corner, and her footsteps stopped.

The slightest noise would give away their hiding place. They held the door closed, their gripping hands squashed side by side in the dark. The officer walked further up the street, radioed that she had lost her targets, turned round and returned to her car.

There was a loud grating noise as Freddy used something heavy to hold the door shut from the inside.

'This way,' he said, and moved off into the dark.

Jac used her hands to guide herself along the musty-smelling wall. With Fabian just behind her, she came to some sort of gate. Freddy was already working on the lock. It swung open with a creak; Jac heard the click of a light switch.

There was an electrical buzz as a chain of fluorescent bulbs kicked into life one by one. A corridor materialised in front of them, and a deep staircase plunged into what looked like infinity. Freddy grabbed Fabian's hand and started to walk down.

'Come on,' he said.

Too tired to say anything, Jac took hold of the bannister rail and followed the boys deep into the underbelly of London.

L

'Wait here,' said Freddy. 'Only the stair lights are connected to mains electricity. I have to start up the generator.' He turned a wheel on a reinforced steel door, heaved it open and disappeared inside.

'*I have to start up the generator*,' mimicked Fabian. 'He sounds like he comes down here all the time.'

'He probably does,' said Jac.

There was a low hum, and the sound of more neon lights pinging into life. Freddy reappeared and gestured for them to join him. They stepped through the doorway into the room beyond.

They were in some sort of hi-tech office. Six desks, in two rows of three, with computer and telecoms equipment. On every desk was a stationery storage unit and a desk lamp. Jac thought it looked like a tableau from a war museum, only without the creepy dummies looking at maps and answering the telephone.

'This is the main ops room,' Freddy said casually. 'Come on, let's go to the kitchen.' He was already halfway out of a door on the far side of the room.

Fabian pulled a face. 'Now he's talking like he piggin' lives here,' he said.

'He probably does,' repeated Jac.

The kitchen was made entirely out of stainless steel, polished and cold. Freddy slid open a cupboard door to reveal a stash of tins.

'What shall we have?' He moved the tins around, reading the labels. 'Beef mince, new potatoes, green beans.' He set them on the work surface with a clang. 'Rice pudding for afters – I think there's some jam somewhere ...'

'Ruddy hell, will you just STOP!' shouted Fabian.

'Sorry – you're right. We should shower first. Get cleaned up before we eat.'

'NO!' Fabian was wild with exasperation. 'What the goofing heck *is* this place? Just tell us!'

Jac laughed. Freddy put the rice pudding down and grinned.

'Welcome to Freddy's hidey-hole number two. A government-made emergency bunker. Used in the Second World War but hushed-up since. Updated regularly – 'just in case'. There's everything you need to live and work if the country goes bosoms-up. I found it by accident six months ago.'

Fabian rubbed his eyes. 'I don't want to know, Fred!'

'Did you say there was a shower?' said Jac. A new layer of sweat and dirt had congealed over her skin and it felt revolting.

'This way,' said Freddy.

A short corridor led to another room with a large communal shower along one wall. Freddy opened a storage trunk and took out towels, and soap wrapped in waxy paper.

'Only cold water, I'm afraid – but we can drink hot chocolate afterwards to warm up.'

He was already taking his clothes off. 'There's only enough in the tank for a five-minute wash.

Takes hours to refill. We have to get in together or two of us will be stinko all night.'

He was naked now, his pale skin tight across his skinny rib cage. Jac turned away, her cheeks burning.

'Fear not, fair maiden,' he said. 'I will sooth your blushes with Shakespeare:

Well could I curse away a winter's night,
Though standing naked on a mountain top,
Where biting cold would never let grass grow,
And think it but a minute spent in sport.'

He leapt in front of her, his willowy limbs gangling, like a little chimpanzee. Jac's cheeks cooled and she smiled, but she still wouldn't look at him.

Letting out a whoop, Freddy darted to the shower and turned a silver lever to release the water. A forceful gush spread outwards from the enormous showerheads and he yelled as it hit his skin. The noise of the water hitting the stainless steel was intense; he screamed and danced as the water bounced off his body and blasted the dirt and soot from his skin, soapsuds sliding off his torso and circling the plughole.

'What are you waiting for, stinkers?' he yelled. 'Water runs out in four minutes!'

Jac had never wanted anyone to see her body. Ever. But her underwear had become melded to her grimy skin and, as she breathed in, she caught a rancid whiff of her own body odour. She was disgusting.

Fabian was laughing and pulling off his clothes. 'Come on,' he grinned. 'Race you!'

Oh, hang it. Jac dragged her top over her head, undid her bra and let it drop to the floor. She removed the rest of her clothes as quickly as she could. Fabian grabbed her hand and they ran into the shower together.

The water was so cold it burned. She squealed like a baby, punching at the jet of water to try and keep it away. The boys cupped their hands and threw fistfuls of water at her, and she splashed them back. Teeth chattering, they huddled close together under the freezing deluge, elbows colliding: fleeting moments of flesh and warmth in a storm of ice.

'Soap! Give me the soap!' Jac washed herself vigorously, rubbing the foam into her hair and body, swearing at the water for being so ruddy freezing and cursing her body for not getting used to the cold.

'Hurry up!' Fabian snatched the soap off her. She massaged her hair to make all the bubbles rinse away. When she looked down she could see the suds coming off her were a vile, yellowy grey.

'My dog's less dirty than you,' said Freddy.

'Shut your face, stick insect!'

Freddy used his arms, volleyball-style, to send a sloosh of water over Jac's body. Fabian flicked a blob of suds at her. Jac tilted her head back, filled her mouth with water and spouted it into the boys' faces.

There was a shuddering noise and the water ran out. Freddy ran to the towels and threw one each to Jac and Fabian. They stood on the wet floor, rubbing the warmth back into their shivering bodies.

'We can't put those filthy clothes on again,' said Fabian. He shared out what he had packed in his bag before they left: tracksuit bottoms and a T-shirt for himself and Fabian. Jac took a jumper and made a sarong for herself out of a dry towel.

Freddy hurried away to make hot chocolate. Her skin still tingling, Jac bobbed up and down to try and get warm.

'This is mad,' she said.

Freddy had started singing like an opera star in the kitchen, and the sound floated through the corridors.

'But I'm glad we're in it together – all three of us, I mean.'

'Me too,' said Fabian.

The sweet scent of cocoa beans wafted in with the music.

'I am *so* hungry,' said Jac.

Fabian murmured in agreement. 'Let's go for it: choccy for starter, yummy tinned mince for main and a bowl of frogspawn for pudding.'

They squeezed through the narrow doorway and out into the corridor. They went into the pristine, silver-coloured kitchen, its walls already dripping with steam as Freddy turned the gas on underneath three hearty-looking saucepans of food.

LI

Jac woke up and stretched out a hand in the dark:
Fabian was not there and the bed was cold. She
rolled over and reached a little further. Instead of
Freddy, there was just a blanket, rough to the skin
and smelling of mothballs. She crawled the length of
the bunk unit and felt for the light switch.

The sleeping bay had three tiers of bunks on either
side of the room, with a narrow gangway in between.
There was room for forty people, squashed side by
side like hens in a multi-storey chicken coop. Jac
tightened her towel-sarong around her waist and
went to the kitchen. Fabian and Freddy were doing
the washing up.

'You've missed breakfast and dinner,' said
Freddy. 'It's half past two.'

Fabian poured some long life orange juice into a
metal mug and gave it to Jac.

'I'll make you a corned beef fritter,' said Fabian.
'Unless you want to go straight for lunch and have
chunked chicken with rice. Or there's porridge made
with water and dried milk.'

'Give me a minute to think about that,' said Jac.
Her stomach writhed; she hadn't woken up enough
to think about food. 'Maybe a cup of tea.'

The kettle bubbled into action, and Fabian finished drying up. Freddy smartened his hair, looking at his reflection in the cupboard doors.

'We need supplies,' he said. 'Clothes and fresh food. And a gas canister for the cooker.'

'I suppose you're going to steal all of this.' Fabian flicked the worktop crossly with his tea towel.

'What else are we to do?' said Freddy. 'We can't use bank cards and there's no cash left. We're fugitives now.'

Fabian said nothing.

'Just don't get caught,' said Jac. 'Come back safe – and soon.'

Freddy pulled on a hoodie and drew it over his face. Some of his hair was showing, so he rubbed gravy powder into it to make it look darker.

'Don't start sweating!' said Jac. 'You'll get gravy-face.'

'I never sweat when I'm on a job,' said Freddy.

He picked up Fabian's sports bag, now empty, and slung it over his shoulder.

'See you kids later,' he said. He blew them a kiss and left the kitchen, the sound of his footsteps disappearing as he headed for the blue metal door that led to the street.

'You really should eat,' said Fabian. 'The tinned chicken's OK – and we saved you some caramel pudding.'

Jac nodded, and Fabian searched in a drawer for a tin opener. He pushed a bag of rice across the worktop, and then he went quiet. As she measured out the rice, Jac knew that it was up to her to break the silence. Her stomach knotted with shame.

'I'm so sorry, Fabian. I was too busy with JASMINE to be a proper friend. Too obsessed. And what I did to your dad ...'

'I'm not ready to talk to you about him,' Fabian snapped. His eyes misted over, he frowned and changed the subject. 'Let's talk about Miss Steele. I don't understand why your portfolio made her so angry. I thought you were her star pupil.'

'So did I,' said Jac. She tipped the rice packet and the grains tumbled into a pan of hot water.

'It all started when I went to Saint Tropez ...'

She told Fabian about being mugged in the ruined streets and meeting Jean-Luc – and the truth about Europe going bust. She described the moment that she found out that Colette was dead. Fabian didn't take his eyes off her as she talked about her decision to use her journalism skills to make sure that Colette's death was not in vain. She recounted her meeting with Richard Masters at the psychiatric hospital, and what the ex-Prime Minister had told her she must do. She said that their flash mob had worked, that people were talking about it on the internet and that there were others out there trying to stop Britain from going bankrupt. Finally she told him that it was JASMINE who had tried to sabotage the flash mob.

'So you see, I wrote the exact opposite of what JASMINE wanted,' she said. 'JASMINE wanted Britain to destroy itself, not make itself better. The moment Miss Steele saw what I'd written, I became the enemy.'

Fabian doodled with his finger on the worktop for what seemed like ages. 'I'm so sorry about Colette,' he said, finally. 'I'm sorry for all of it.'

'So can you see, I had my reasons for ...?'

'I do not want to talk to you about my dad.' Fabian turned away to stir the chicken and Jac watched the spoon as it moved unforgivingly around the saucepan.

'There is more,' she said. 'But I'll tell you later.'

Fabian nodded, and they finished preparing the meal. There was a small canteen next door, with a television in the corner. Jac ate; they slumped in front of the TV, watching quizzes and daytime cookery shows, until tiredness crept over her again. She put her head down on the table and, after a while, the sounds from the screen became muffled and distant. When she woke up again, Fabian was asleep beside her, his hair dipping into the leftover chicken sauce. The news was on the TV.

'Concern is growing for the safety of Fabian Traves, the son of the former Home Secretary. 14-year-old Fabian went missing yesterday along with two school friends, both of whom are wanted for questioning by the police and social services ...'

Jac switched off the TV and bit her nails. In the silence, she could hear a muffled banging echoing through the corridors. Fabian stirred, lifted his head and stared at Jac.

'What's that?' He looked at his watch: it was twenty to seven. 'Where's Fred? The shops shut ages ago.'

The banging got louder.

'Oh, heck. Do you think it's the police?'

'Sheesh.' Fabian scratched his head.

Jac went to the door and listened. 'Freddy would never tell them where we are, not in a million years.'

'Should we hide?' said Fabian.

'You can – I'm curious,' said Jac.

She slipped off in the direction of the banging, past the sleeping bay and along a passageway they had not used before. Halfway down, there were no more bulbs in the light sockets and she walked slowly, feeling her way along the corridor.

'Wait for me,' breathed Fabian. The banging increased and Jac quickened her pace.

The knocking was now very close. Beneath Jac's hands, the bricks gave way to a sheet of metal.

'There's a door here!'

Somebody shouted. It was Freddy. Fabian joined Jac as she grasped the wheel-shaped door handle, and they both spun it round in the dark. There was a clunk, and they heaved the door inwards. A beam of light spilled into the corridor and Freddy emerged, a torch in his teeth and carrier bags brimming in each hand.

'What kept you? I've been knocking for ages.' He dumped the bags on the floor and took the torch out of his mouth. 'I had two store detectives and a squad car after me. My arms are killing me.'

Jac peered into the tunnel that stretched out beyond the door. 'Where does this go?'

'An old tube station, amongst other places,' said Freddy. 'Are you going to help me carry this stuff, or what?'

They re-sealed the door and took the bags to the canteen. Freddy was wearing different clothes now, and he seemed a lot fatter.

'We're in all the papers,' said Freddy as he unpacked food, more clothes and a gas canister. 'The cops recognised me straight away.'

He felt beneath his top, pulled out several newspapers and put them on the table. 'They would have caught me if there hadn't been a mob of people on Regent Street.' He took two bars of chocolate out of one of his sleeves. 'Some anti-government thing. The SuperSavings Alliance? I ran into the crowd and the cops lost me.'

Jac unfolded one of the papers.

'Piggin' heck,' she said. She showed Fabian the front page.

THE DAILY WOW!
PROTESTER THROWS SOUP AT ECONOMIC SECRETARY

David Pearson, Economic Secretary to the Treasury, was drenched in vegetable soup yesterday by a man protesting against what he called 'the government's sickening approach to Britain's finances' ...

'Dad was at school with the editor of the *Daily Wow!*' said Fabian. 'They've *never* printed anything against the government before.'

'Maybe things really are changing,' said Jac.

Freddy reached into another bag and pulled out a pair of designer jogging trousers in Jac's size, a 3-pack of knickers and a biker-style top. 'Let's get you out of that awful towel, Jac.'

'They're green!' Jac turned the clothes over in her hands.

'Emerald. And you will look fabulous in it. Trust me. Oh, and here's some cream for your skin.'

Jac took the clothes and ointment into the sleeping bay. Before she changed, she dabbed the cream into the sores on her hips and shoulders, wincing as the antiseptic came into contact with her raw flesh. Once dressed, she took a detour to the washroom to see what she looked like, edging towards the mirror like a nervous kitten. Annoyingly, Freddy was right: the colour did suit her. It seemed to put something back into her face and make it look – prettier. Hesitantly, she raised her hands to her hairline and rearranged her curls a little. Then, feeling stupid, she turned away from her reflection and hurried back to the mess room.

As she walked in, the boys were hunched over one of the papers and talking in low voices.

'What is it?' Jac tried to take the newspaper from Fabian but he pulled it away.

'Maybe you should sit down.' He was looking at her weirdly.

'Don't be such a wussy – why should I?'

Freddy looked at Fabian. Fabian bit his lip.

'Stop acting like idiots, you two.' Jac snatched the paper from Fabian and scanned the front page. In the bottom right hand corner was a short article.

Lawyers Missing
Top legal duo Flick Stryder and Julian Jones are presumed dead, after their burnt-out car was found at the bottom of a ravine in Arizona, USA yesterday. They were holidaying in America and were due to return to Britain next week. Their daughter, Jacqueline, is also missing and is wanted by police in connection with a string of minor offences.
It is not clear if the two disappearances are connected.

'Cripes. Sorry,' said Fabian.

Freddy looked at the floor.

'Don't talk to me,' Jac muttered. She felt as if she had been punched in the stomach. She picked up the newspaper, clutched it to her chest and ran out of the room.

LII

Jac ripped through the printed pages, searching for more information. 'This can't be true,' she said.

Fabian had followed her into the ops room. He stared at her.

'My parents are *not* dead,' she said. 'The great Flick and Julian beaten by death?' She laughed. 'They'd have paid death to shut up and go away.'

There were footsteps and Freddy put his head round the door.

'And if they *are* ...' Jac scrunched up an unwanted sheet and tossed it onto the floor. 'Well, they can't mess me up anymore, can they?'

Freddy looked at her uneasily. 'I've put the kettle on,' he said.

'Thanks,' said Jac. 'Tea's good.' She clicked her fingers impatiently. 'But first, I want to tell you the rest of my story.'

'Are you sure, babes?' Fabian touched her on the arm.

'Yes. I'm a hard-hearted cow, remember?'

She told them about God's Profiteers. She spoke about the mysterious hiding-place called Glenoustie Croft, that the Profiteers had done some sort of deal with the British government – and that her mum and dad were involved. She recounted Daniel Bavington's bizarre decision to protect her parents and expose his own embarrassing story to the press instead. And she finished with JASMINE going to the mental health hospital and abducting and murdering Richard Masters.

Freddy got up and dragged his chair to a nearby desk. He switched on the computer.

'Right – let's sort out these connections once and for all.' He touch-typed swiftly, the keyboard purring with a continuous stream of high-speed clicks. 'The government, God's Profiteers, Jac's parents ... and JASMINE. It's all in here somewhere.'

The British government website appeared on the screen.

'We don't know the password,' said Jac.

'Sometimes you can guess it,' said Freddy, his fingers moving like spiders across the keys. 'Come on, guys, help me out! Politicians are arrogant – they pick passwords that show off their successes. What's the government done recently?'

'Soup Kitchen Bill?' said Jac. 'Free soup for anyone with an income less than £40,000 a year.'

Freddy tried 'freesoup', 'soupbill', '40Ksoup', 'soupforthepoor', 'soupfortherich' and many more.

'Dad got the law changed so everyone could have those mini pools ...' said Fabian.

Freddy spun round in his chair. 'That's it, Fabe! Your dad! He's the key!' His eyes gleamed. 'What's his government password?'

'The only thing I know is that he could never remember them,' said Fabian. 'So he used an online password safe.'

'Which company?'

'StrongBox UK, I think.'

Freddy found StrongBox UK's website. 'What's your dad's email address?'

Fabian typed it in.

'OK. So, your dad's forgetful, right?' said Freddy. 'Password safes won't let you change your access ID. So your dad had to choose something easy to remember so he couldn't get locked out.'

Fabian's face spread into a grin. 'Try *Jonian*. Half my brother's name, half me.'

'Won't Fabian's dad's password be out of date now?' said Jac.

'Doubt it.' Freddy typed it in. He clicked the mouse and a graphic of a golden key slowly rotated in the centre of the screen.

'Come on ... come on ...' The key turned red and started flashing. 'What the ...?'

Jac couldn't bear to look. She covered her face and heard Freddy thump his fist on the desk.

'Bingo! We're IN!'

A list of Barnaby Traves's passcodes to all areas of the government website shone from the computer.

Freddy logged on and began to search. As he typed, Jac and Fabian went to the canteen to make the tea.

'Might have known he'd be a computer hacker as well,' said Fabian.

'Yeah – he's a right little criminal.' Jac peeled the foil from one of the large hazelnut bars Freddy had shoplifted, broke off a big chunk and gave it to Fabian. 'But we couldn't have done this without him.'

Fabian smiled. He shoved all eight squares of the chocolate into his mouth at once, and it bulged out through both his cheeks. Jac pushed an even bigger slab into her mouth and tried to talk, but she had lost all her consonants.

'I gheg your ghardon?' said Fabian.

Jac laughed and sprayed liquid chocolate all over the kettle.

They made the tea and returned to the ops room. Jac waved some chocolate under Freddy's nose to see if he wanted some. Freddy stopped typing and clutched his forehead.

'Oh my God.' He turned the monitor so that they could see it. 'Firstly, it looks like God's Profiteers are about to invade Germany. They've basically enslaved half of Europe. But that's nothing compared to what I've just found.' He opened up a new tab. 'This is it. This is the deal. This is what they've done.'

Jac and Fabian stared at the screen.

It couldn't be clearer. Three weeks ago, the government had agreed to sell the whole of Britain to God's Profiteers at the knockdown price of three hundred million pounds.

It was less than five pounds per person.

LIII

The truth was out. The British government, knowing that the country was going bankrupt, had sold their own people to God's Profiteers for slave labour. Jac's parents had helped broker the deal. The three hundred million pounds would keep the government (and other 'important' people) in luxury in Glenoustie Croft, whilst the rest of the nation starved.

Jac, Fabian and Freddy drank their tea and talked in low voices.

'I'm not sure Britain is ready to hear this,' said Jac. 'It's so crazy people will think it's a lie.'

'I agree,' said Fabian. 'Dad said it was always the stupid little stories that made the headlines, not the important ones.'

'So let's flood the country with stupid little stories, then,' said Freddy. 'Just like Richard Masters wanted you to, Jac.'

Jac felt a weight of sadness press on her chest. She hoped Masters would have been proud of her.

They sat at a computer each. Between them they created multiple email accounts, and used them to set up scores of false identities on all the main social network sites.

'We need to blitz the internet with trivial anti-government posts,' said Freddy. 'Don't just write single messages: create conversations between your fake identities and wait for people to join in. Let's get everyone moaning about the government!'

They worked all night. By the next morning the internet was buzzing with soundbites and questions, and a minor radio station hosted a phone-in about whether the government could be trusted.

But by lunchtime it was clear that their internet conversations were being erased faster than they could create them. The government was deleting everything.

Jac threw a pen across the room and slumped into a demoralised silence.

'We can't do it,' said Freddy. 'There just aren't enough of us.'

'We can't just give up,' said Fabian.

Freddy got up and kicked his chair over with a clatter. He stalked into the canteen and put the radio on at full volume. Angry punk music reverberated through the bunker and Fabian, shaking his head, walked out along the corridor and disappeared into the darkness. Jac went to the kitchen and sat on the worktop, swinging her heels against the stainless steel door.

The punk music raved on and on. Finally the music broke for the hourly news and a woman's voice blared into the room.

'... Anger is growing after the Education Secretary was overheard insulting a grieving dog owner and his much-loved dog. The Right Honourable Patricia Evans accidently ran over a Yorkshire terrier whilst out shopping earlier today. Cookie the dog was seriously injured and Mrs Evans apologised to the owner. But she was

overheard joking later that both the owner – eighty-nine year old Wilfred White – and his dog should be put down ...'

Freddy ran into the kitchen. 'Did you hear that? Did you hear it? They won't be able to shut us up this time - there'll be *millions* of people complaining! A poor little hard-done-by doggie! What an amazing stroke of luck!'

'Of course I heard it,' grinned Jac.

Fabian came racing through the door to the ops room, hit the nearest keyboard and let out a whoop. *#JusticeForCookie* was already trending on *dinkytalk*.

They rushed back to the computers, joining in with the avalanche of angry cries that was swamping the internet.

By teatime, *#JusticeForCookie* was the number one topic across the web. On Monday morning, Patricia Evans resigned in disgrace.

On Tuesday, a drive-time radio show told its listeners to stop their cars for five minutes in support of Cookie. Helicopter footage showed hundreds of thousands of dangerously parked cars forcing the roads into gridlock, right across the country.

The British Transport Union immediately called a national strike, saying they were concerned for the safety of their bus and taxi drivers. On Wednesday, the railway workers agreed to support them. Two days later, the teachers' unions – angry at the government for setting a bad example to children – said they, too, would strike, and force thousands of schools to close. It looked like the whole British workforce might stop working.

Jac leant back in her chair and looked at Freddy and Fabian. They were both smiling.

'This is it, isn't it?' said Jac. 'This is the right

moment!'

'Ha ha! Cookie the dog – we love you!' said Fabian.

Freddy rolled up his sleeves. He had already drafted an email exposing the government's treacherous deal with God's Profiteers.

'Send it,' said Fabian. 'Britain is ready.'

Freddy stood up, his hand poised melodramatically over the mouse. 'Time to make a big noise ...' he said.

There was a loud bang.

A solid wall of air blasted through the room. Jac and Fabian were knocked off their chairs and Freddy flew backwards into the wall. Out in the corridor, the sound of falling debris resonated like heavy rain. Then, as the fragments settled and a thin mist of smoke leaked into the room, two pairs of prowling footsteps came towards them. Fabian lifted Jac to her feet and stumbled through the chairs to help Freddy.

'This way,' urged Freddy – but it was too late.

Two masked men burst through the ops room door. The whites of their eyes, staring robotically through the slits in their balaclavas, flashed around the room. One of the men stared at Jac. The other fixed a calculated gaze first on Freddy, and then Fabian.

Without speaking, one of them gave a signal. They lifted their machine guns to hip height and opened fire.

LIV

There was a smash, and the room was plunged into darkness. Red-hot bullet traces cut through the air and the two guns rattled, sending shards of computer screen and bits of plaster bouncing round the room. As Jac dived to the ground, she thought she remembered Freddy throwing something at the light bulb, but she couldn't be sure.

She felt a hand squeeze her ankle: her heart flipped – one of the boys was still alive, at least. Then the bullets stopped.

'Did we get them?' said a cold voice.

There was a scuffle on the other side of the room and another smash. The fire alarm went off and a deluge of water poured into the room from the sprinklers. Somebody crawled on top of her and shouted into her ear, the words barely audible over the ringing of the alarm bell.

'Come with me.'

It sounded like Freddy, which meant that it was Fabes holding her leg. She reached down and took Fabian's hand, signalling with a squeeze that he should hold on tight. She grasped Freddy's hoodie, and the three of them slid across the floor towards the kitchen.

Two streams of light flashed, criss-crossing around the room. The masked men shouted at each other, but the alarm drowned their voices and the water from the sprinklers broke up the light from their torches. The killers searched in vain, and Jac and the boys slithered out of the room. They crouched in the unlit kitchen, water streaming over them.

'Who are they?' Jac's teeth chattered as she spoke.

'Whoever they are, when they realise they haven't killed us, they're going to follow us in here.' By the faint light of the oven clock, Jac could see Freddy opening a cupboard. He tugged at Jac's sleeve.

'Through the hatch at the back,' he shouted. 'Straight ahead for fifty metres.'

Jac crawled through a small, square hole and into a narrow shaft beyond. Behind her, the boys scrabbled on their hands and knees. The noise of the alarm faded, and she could hear their wet clothes shuffling across the concrete.

'There's a bend to the right,' said Freddy. 'Any minute now.'

The tunnel widened and it was possible to stand up. Freddy moved off into the dark. There was the sound of a handle turning, and dim light leaked in from a bigger tunnel beyond.

'Where now?' The pale light shone on Fabian's face as he spoke.

'Wait,' said Freddy. He stood still and listened. 'They must have figured out that we're not dead by now.'

A roar rumbled from behind and a huge cloud of concrete dust whooshed around them. They choked, grit penetrating their lungs and stinging their eyes.

'They've blown up the escape shaft,' coughed

Freddy. 'They're trying to flush us out.'

With nowhere else to run, they jumped into the main corridor. The two killers burst through a door at the far end and opened fire. Jac ran for her life, the boys' feet pounding behind her. But the assassins' machine guns were fired in vain: the tunnel was steeply curved and the bullets bounced off the brickwork without tasting flesh.

Freddy pushed ahead round the corner, and used his lock-picking tool to open a door in the wall. The three of them piled inside, and Freddy manipulated the lock again. Outside, the gunmen raced past and their footsteps faded.

'Lost them. But not for long,' said Freddy. His clothes dripped on the floor as he walked away in the dark. He rummaged for a few moments, then a torch flicked on, its yellow light shining eerily on his face.

'There's another one here. Who wants it?'

Fabian took it and shone the light this way and that, and Jac tried to make sense of the fragments she was seeing. On the wall was a red ring bisected with a horizontal blue stripe that contained the words:

GREYCOAT STREET

'London Underground Station. Built in 1910, never opened to the public,' said Freddy. 'No time to stop, though. Follow me.'

Another explosion rumbled behind them. A plug of compressed air whistled through the corridors and hit them in the back.

'These guys are getting boring now,' said Jac.

They quickened their pace, skidding round the corners of the passages and stairways. As they descended the stairs, old-fashioned adverts for soap, exhibitions, tinned milk and marmalade clung to the wall tiles, their colours vividly preserved in the dark.

Eventually the three of them arrived at the northbound platform, and sprinted towards the exit at the other end. Then two beams of light sprayed out in front of them. With a triumphant shout, the masked men burst from a far corridor, their white teeth snarling in the half-light.

'Jump!' screamed Freddy.

Without slowing down, the three of them leapt sideways into the darkness. Bullets snapped at their heels as they flew through the air and landed on the tracks. As they hit the ground, Fabian let out an agonised squeal. His torch tumbled to the ground and the light went out.

'No! No! NO!' wailed Freddy.

Jac grabbed Fabian's right arm and felt Freddy tug at the other. 'Has he been shot?' Her heart was in her throat.

'My ankle ...' Fabian's voice was riddled with pain.

'Hop! You have to, baby!'

Fabian draped his arm around Jac's neck and they stumbled into the tunnel, Fabian gasping with every step they took.

The gunfire had stopped. There was a thud as the two assassins landed on the track behind them. Fabian was getting heavier and heavier. They struggled to get away, and the two pairs of footsteps thumped nearer.

'Come on guys, we can do it,' said Jac.

But a hand gripped her and jerked her backwards. Taken off balance, Fabian slipped to the ground. The second gunman snatched at Freddy and pinned his arms behind his back. Freddy's torch was taken from him and thrown into the depths of the tunnel with a clatter, the light dying as it hit the ground.

Jac's captor flung her against the tunnel wall. Freddy was thrown beside her. A torch was shone in their faces and, behind the bright light, Jac heard Fabian yelp as he was picked up off the tunnel floor. Then he, too, slammed into the wall with a thud. She slipped her hand into his. To her left, she reached out and felt for Freddy's fingers. They entwined around hers.

A second torch shone in their faces. 'Turn around,' said a voice.

With a heaving heart, Jac let Fabian and Freddy go. 'Goodbye,' she breathed, and turned to face the brickwork. It smelt of soot.

'Hands above your heads against the wall.'

She moved her arms as slowly as she dared. Freddy was silent; Fabian breathed in sobs.

'Who told you to do this? Who sent you?' Her shouts echoed down the tunnel like a tiny, lost child calling for her mum.

One of the gunmen laughed. 'Shoot her first. Then the boys.'

There was a long pause. Like cats, the killers were enjoying taunting their prey. Fabian snivelled and Freddy let out a moan. Tears leaked out of Jac's eyes and splashed down her cheeks.

The gunmen primed their weapons with a click that reverberated down the tunnel and into infinity.

Jac held her breath and waited to die.

LV

A deep droning sound penetrated the tunnel. There was a flash and a bang. The two gunmen screamed and the sound ripped through the air. Something crackled and thumped behind them and a putrid-smelling smoke entered Jac's nostrils.

She daren't turn round, instead feeling for Freddy and Fabian and pulling them closer to her. She kept her head down, still expecting to be torn apart by a shower of searing bullets. It was horribly quiet. Then there was a low buzz, and the atmosphere in the tunnel seemed to shift.

Back at the station platform, somebody dropped down onto the track and walked slowly towards them. The beam from a flashlight bobbed up and down, scanning from left to right as it approached.

'Hello?' The footsteps came nearer.

'Who is it?' Jac swallowed hard: was this still part of the killers' sick game?

'Jac, is that you?' The voice sounded relieved. And familiar. 'Are you ok?'

How did he know her name? 'We're all fine, I think. Just a broken ankle.'

The flashlight traced across them, and the rescuer stepped forward. 'Thank God you're all right.'

A hand touched her shoulder. She turned to look. Standing in a mixture of light and shadow was Gary the receptionist.

Her head spinning with surprise, she allowed him to hug her. Gary shook the boys' hands, checking they were ok with a deft sweep of the torch, then moved to where the gunmen had been standing. All that remained of them were two blackened bodies sprawled across the tracks.

'What happened to them?' The spotlight picked out a charred and bloody arm and Jac turned away.

'I switched on the live rail,' said Gary. He started to search the corpses. 'It was a risk. I could have killed you at the same time. But I'd run out of options. A second later and you'd have been dead anyway.'

He found a mobile phone on one of the bodies, and put it in his pocket.

'A week ago, we intercepted a call from Penelope Steele. We heard her contact JASMINE and order Jac's execution. So we mobilised a rescue party. We had you in our sights, Jac, but we lost you after the kidnap attempt.'

He continued to raid the gunmen's pockets. 'Then we detected somebody hacking into government websites and we backed a hunch that it was you. We traced the computer activity to the Greycoat Street ops room. Unfortunately, JASMINE traced you there too.'

Jac watched him as he completed his search. He had just saved her life. For a moment, she felt completely in love with him. Then, infuriated by such feelings, she shook herself and turned to Fabian and Freddy.

'This is Gary,' she said.

LVI

The gunman's phone still worked. Gary thumbed the keypad, trying to find out who had sent the order to kill. He was squashed close beside Jac, and she could feel the muscles in his arm twitching as he pressed the buttons.

Opposite her, Fabian slumped, half asleep. Gary had given him some painkillers from a first aid pack and he seemed more relaxed. Freddy watched Gary as he fiddled with the phone.

'Gotcha,' said Gary. The phone beeped and he sent the word '*Done*' with his thumb. He removed the SIM card from the phone, took out a cigarette lighter and held the card in the flame until it nearly burnt his fingers. Snapping the lighter shut, he dropped the smouldering SIM on the van floor.

'Toolbox,' he said, gesturing to Jac to reach for a metal case in the corner of the van. He took out a hammer and beat the SIM card until it shattered. Then he scooped up the pieces and put them in his pocket.

'I've sent JASMINE confirmation that you've been killed. Message sent, phones destroyed, gunmen have disappeared, as agreed. As far as JASMINE is concerned, the job was a success.'

'But won't they hear about the bodies in the tunnel?' said Freddy.

'No,' said Gary. 'Greycoat Street is protected by the Official Secrets Act. The government will dispose of the corpses.'

Fabian murmured drowsily, and Freddy patted his hand.

'How exactly does JASMINE fit into all this?' asked Jac. 'That's the bit we couldn't work out.'

'JASMINE is working for God's Profiteers.'

The van's diesel engine rattled as they stopped at a junction, and a group of drunken women walked past outside, singing.

'JASMINE hires out teenage guerrillas to anyone that wants them. God's Profiteers paid JASMINE to sabotage Britain. When the country was weak enough, the Profiteers were going to storm in and take over. But it didn't go to plan: the SuperSavings Alliance got support, and it was possible that Britain would save itself. The Profiteers were angry and told JASMINE to mobilise more teenagers to stop the SuperSavings Alliance. That's why JASMINE brought this year's portfolio deadline forward.'

'Does the government know that JASMINE is using kids to destroy the country?'

'Yes – and they want JASMINE to succeed. That way it won't look like it's the government's fault when Britain collapses and God's Profiteers move in.'

'So what are we waiting for?' said Freddy. 'We've got everything we need to expose the government and stop the Profiteers invading! Have you got computers where we're going?'

'We've got a team working on that,' said Gary. 'But it's all about timing.'

The van had stopped. The driver got out and

opened the back doors. They were parked in a back alley somewhere; ill-lit and reeking of unemptied bins. There was jazz music coming from nearby. The smell of hot cooking fat wafted from an open window.

'This way,' said Gary.

Fabian had fallen asleep, so Gary picked him up and carried him over his shoulder. They walked to a fire exit. Gary knocked twice; somebody opened it from the inside and they all stepped into a dark, smoke-stained stairwell that smelt of beer and sweat.

The sound of a jazz band danced upwards, and Gary led them downstairs into the basement of the building.

LVII

A door swung open and a carnival of music burst out. Six instruments played simultaneously, the melodies jumping and jiving with each other, driven by a jazzy drum beat.

Fabian woke up. Gary set him down in the doorway and waited for him to get his bearings. Then they walked through the bar.

The club was packed with people. They swayed to the music, tapping their feet or beating out the rhythm with their fingers on the tables. The bar, lit with the words *'Slick Harry's'* in purple neon, was buzzing. Customers wove through the tables with glasses of beer, white foam slipping down the sides. The rainbow lights on the dance floor bounced from wall to wall like a shower of candies.

Gary took them to the green room behind the stage, where a man was waiting for them.

'Fabian, this is Hodge,' said Gary. 'He will look after you.'

Hodge pulled a wheelchair from behind an old synthesizer. 'You're going to need an X-ray for that leg. There's a car waiting at the front of the building to take you to a private hospital. We'll sort you out with dry clothes when you get there.'

'Can I go with him?' asked Freddy.

'Of course,' said Hodge. 'They'll check you over as well.'

Gary spoke quietly to Jac. 'We'll need to see you're OK, too, but I want to show you something first.'

Freddy and Hodge pushed Fabian in the wheelchair to a service lift, and the door closed behind them. Gary took Jac through a door in the far corner. There was another room beyond, lit by a single, bare bulb which cast huge, sloping shadows on the walls. A low archway on the right led to another area, and Jac could make out a row of old hospital beds and a chipped sink in the corner.

'I always wanted to stay at the piggin' Ritz,' she said.

Gary laughed. 'We never stay in the same place long.' He touched her hand, and her blood fizzed round her body like champagne. 'But hopefully this is our final destination. Jac, there's somebody I want you to meet.'

He waved towards the corner and Jac peered into the shadows. She hadn't noticed before, but there was somebody sitting there.

It was a man in his fifties. He had a beard and, when Jac squinted, she could see that he was wearing a checked shirt and a corduroy baker boy cap. He looked like one of the jazz crowd from the club, and Jac wondered what he was doing in the back room.

He was smiling at her, his eyes catching a thread of light from the naked bulb. He got up and stepped forward.

'Hello, Jac. It's so nice to see you again.'

With a leap of her heart, she recognised his voice immediately. It was Richard Masters. Unable to stop herself, she launched into his arms, hugging him tightly around his neck. Masters lifted her off the ground and kissed her on the cheek.

'I thought they'd killed you,' she said, blinking her tears away.

'Fortunately, this lot arrived at the Institute before JASMINE,' he said. 'They took me to a private clinic, and they've been helping me get better. Then they brought me here yesterday.'

'Look, Jac,' said Gary. He pointed to a doorway that was obscured by a curtain. Through a gap in the fabric, Jac could see a team of people working at computers.

'The Black Rats are campaigning twenty-four hours a day. We've just been waiting for Richard to get strong again. Then we remove this government and put Richard and his team back in.'

'And I can shave off this ridiculous beard.' Masters' eyes twinkled brighter and he sat down again. 'A cup of cocoa, perhaps?' he said to Gary.

Gary disappeared through another curtain into a kitchen.

'So, Jac,' said Masters. 'Why don't you get changed and then you can tell me about all the clever things you've been up to since we last met.'

*

Gary held out a third cup of cocoa. 'We should think about turning in,' he said. 'Try and get a couple of hours' sleep at least.'

Whilst Jac had been talking to Masters, Fabian and Freddy had returned from the private hospital. The X-ray had shown that Fabian's ankle muscles were badly torn, but nothing was broken. He had been given more painkillers and the ankle had been packed in ice and then dressed. He and Freddy had gone straight to bed, choosing two beds next to each other and falling asleep side by side.

Masters had begun to look a little faded, and he excused himself and headed for the bed next to Freddy's. Within minutes he was snoring gently. Jac stared after him, watching his sleeping body for a while.

'You ok?' said Gary. He perched himself on the arm of Jac's chair.

Jac shrugged. 'When I was talking to him ... he actually seemed ... proud of me.'

Gary punched her gently on the arm. 'We're all proud of you. You've been amazing.'

'Piggin' heck.' She turned to look at him and smiled. 'No-one's been interested in me all my life and now I get two massive compliments in one day. What a laugh.'

She punched him back, expecting him to respond with one of his jokes about her being a deranged teenage nutbag. But his expression changed and he leant forward and kissed her. Her heart danced as his fingers caught a few curls of her hair and held them for a while. Then he backed off and stood up.

'I'm sorry,' he said.

Without knowing where she got her confidence from, Jac sprang from her chair, threaded her arms around Gary's neck and, standing on tiptoe, kissed him back. She felt his hands press into her shoulder blades as he held her, his forearms in close contact with her ribs. The front of her body melted into his, their heartbeats competing with each other to see which was the fastest. For several long moments, she felt as if she didn't exist in her own right. She and

Gary were particles in a perfect universe and nothing else mattered.

He pulled away from her gently, sliding his arms round so that he held her just above the elbows. He sighed.

'I shouldn't have done that.'

Jac felt herself going pink. 'Oh yeah. You've got a girlfriend.'

'No, I haven't. I was tailing Penelope Steele that day you saw me in my van. I had to say something so I didn't blow my cover.'

'Oh.'

'With everything that's gone on, I'd forgotten how young you are. That's what I mean.'

'I'm fourteen!'

'Exactly. I'm eighteen.'

'That doesn't matter!'

'Actually, it does.' He caressed her arms kindly. 'It does matter.'

The warm feeling that had been coursing through her body started to leak out of her. She tried to keep her face neutral but could feel it warping into an expression of disappointment. He saw the change and kissed her lightly on the cheek.

'When I heard the death threat on you, I realised how much you meant to me. I thought of the world without this brave, mad, weird girl in it – and it felt terrible.' His fingers interlocked with hers. 'So I'm not going to let you go now.' He caressed her hair again. 'We're going to be so busy over the next couple of years putting the country to rights that we won't have time for all the soppy stuff. When we've finished saving the planet we can think about being together. What do you reckon?'

She nearly swooned. Her and Gary, working side

by side to change the world. And he liked her so much he was prepared to wait for her. She felt her lips blossom into a gooey smile and she didn't care what it looked like.

'We need to sleep,' he said.

Jac chose the bed nearest the wall and lay down on top of the covers. It was a hot night and the room was poorly ventilated. She turned on to her side and closed her eyes. As she started to fall asleep, she heard the bed next to her creak as Gary, too, turned in for the night.

Upstairs in the club, the jazz party was still going strong. The sound of the deeper instruments was muted now, but the clarinet and trumpet could still be heard. The two melodies danced around each other, perfectly entwined: a joyous, ebony-coloured thread weaving around a liquid strand of gold.

From the sound of his breathing, Gary had fallen asleep instantly. The jazz notes continued to swirl around them, and Jac drifted into a deep and blissful sleep.

LVIII

The Black Rats crowded around a single computer. With a click of the mouse, a woman called Sheila sent emails to news agencies around the world, revealing the shocking truth that the British government was prepared to sell its citizens – for less than five pounds each – as slaves.

A spontaneous cheer erupted from the group. Richard Masters – now clean-shaven and wearing a new suit – shook everyone's hand in turn. Hodge handed round a mismatched collection of old mugs and poured a slug of sparkling wine into each.

'Cheers!'

The other computers had rolling news stations on the screen, and everybody positioned themselves to watch.

'How long?' asked Hodge.

'I reckon less than ten minutes,' said Gary.

Freddy set his stopwatch.

'And which channel first?' said Jac.

'We should take bets,' said Fabian.

It took six minutes. The news broke in America first, the words running along the bottom of the screen in capital letters. Then a BBC newsreader was handed a piece of paper live on air and the station went into overdrive. Within twenty minutes, every single television channel had stopped their programmes and was broadcasting news flashes. The social networking sites crashed. Music was wiped from the radio stations and replaced with wall-to-wall talk.

'There's going to be a riot,' said Jac.

But she was wrong.

People walked out into the street. They left their homes, their jobs, their schools, and stepped into the sunshine. TV footage from around the country showed the same thing: hundreds of people standing still, strangers holding hands with strangers, friends and colleagues talking in low voices ... or saying nothing at all.

It was as if everybody needed to have a good, long look at what they had nearly lost.

Sky News was the first to show pictures of a fleet of police cars screeching into Downing Street. The Acting Deputy Commissioner of the Metropolitan Police held up a warrant for the arrest of the Prime Minister and his cabinet. The door to Number Ten was opened; the police moved swiftly inside. A crowd gathered at the gates and, as the disgraced government members were brought out in handcuffs, a slow handclap resonated down the street. As the police cars drove off, the people at the gates turned their backs in silent disgust.

'Are you ready?' Hodge put his hand on Masters' shoulder.

The beds in the sleeping area had been pushed to one side, and bright lights and a video camera installed. A single, decrepit armchair had been placed in front of the bare brick wall.

'Time to broadcast to the nation.' Masters winked

at Jac and took his place in the chair.

'It doesn't look very statesman-like,' whispered Fabian.

'No, it's perfect,' said Jac. 'People will compare it to the disgusting luxury of Glenoustie Croft and fall in love with Masters all over again.'

'Fall in love with him like you have, you mean.' Fabian nudged her.

'Shut up.' She elbowed him in the ribs. But it was true.

'Quiet, please,' said Hodge.

With the Black Rats gathered behind the camera, Masters composed himself.

'Five, four ...' Hodge continued the countdown silently on his fingers; the 'record' light glowed like a red-hot pinprick; Masters lifted his head and looked straight down the lens of the camera.

It only lasted five minutes, but his speech was electric. Masters had no script and no autocue. Finally, his words were being heard. Jac flicked a tear from the corner of one eye; Gary slipped his arm around her and hugged her.

'... And the question is, what happens now?' The camera zoomed in on Masters for a close-up. 'It's going to be difficult. It's going to be painful for a long, long time. But if we want our beautiful Britain back ... this is the price we have to pay.'

He didn't even blink.

'Richness and wealth is not just about money. We must remember that in the coming months. We can find prosperity in the strength of our communities, the closeness of our friends – and in the joy and simplicity of our own hearts. Thank you for listening.'

The 'record' light went off and there was silence.

'Was that ok?' said Masters. 'Should we go again?'

Somebody shouted 'Bravo', and applause swelled around the room.

'That was amazing,' said Freddy. 'I wish I could give a speech like that.'

Hodge was already uploading the video onto the computer, ready to broadcast on OurClipz. Everybody knew it was only a matter of minutes before the news networks would be showing the footage.

'I think I've found another bottle of something,' said Masters.

There was a loud 'pop' as he pulled out the cork. The Black Rats crowded round to re-fill their mugs ... and then they waited.

LIX

Two hours after the speech first hit the internet, Richard Masters was taken in the white van to Whitehall for emergency talks with the remaining members of the government. With him were supporters from the SuperSavings Alliance. The Civil Contingencies Act was implemented to prevent rioting and chaos. New laws were rushed through and Masters was reinstated as Prime Minister, without opposition.

Back in the jazz club basement, the Black Rats were dispersing.

'Are you ready, guys?' said Gary. 'We need to move.'

Jac, Fabian and Freddy were sitting in the green room.

'We'll go on foot,' said Gary. 'Get some food and have a debrief. Then we can get you back to your families.'

Jac's innards knotted. What family? A dead one? Or a horrible one. Either way, she didn't want it.

They said goodbye to Hodge and walked out through the empty club. They climbed the stairs to the street and walked unnoticed amongst the crowds gathering on the pavement. Gary took them to a block of flats a couple of miles away. They took the lift to the eleventh floor and slipped along the corridors. With a jangle of keys, Gary unlocked one of the uniformly beige front doors and let them inside.

'I'll go and get breakfast. Any requests?'

'Fresh juice,' said Jac.

'Real bacon,' said Fabian.

'Proper milk,' said Freddy.

Gary smiled. 'I'll be back soon,' he said, and disappeared.

The three of them sat on the sofa and switched on the television.

News was coming through that the JASMINE buildings had been raided and the college Principal arrested. A mosaic of photographs flashed onto the screen: kids from JASMINE who were wanted by the police. Then a new photo appeared: Penelope Steele's eyes looked daggers at the camera and her lipstick glared blood red. 'Do not approach this woman,' said the newsreader. 'She may be armed.'

'Do you think she'll come after you?' said Freddy.

'She's mad enough,' said Jac.

She went over to the window, looking down at the tiny cars and people swarming between the buildings. The city looked like an ants' nest that had been disturbed: streams of people spilling out onto the streets and moving as one. Resting her chin on one hand, she leant on the window sill and watched the changing patterns below.

Later, Gary returned from the supermarket. When he saw the television on, he frowned. He switched it off and went to the kitchen. He unpacked the bags and, not long afterwards, there was a loud double-tap at the front door. Gary opened it.

'Everyone, this is David,' he said.   'He's a psychologist and will be carrying out the debrief.'

'Sounds a bit dramatic,' said Fabian.

'You've been through a lot,' said Gary.   'David will assess if you're ok.'

David nodded. 'Some of the things you have seen cannot be shared. I'm here to help you with your cover story: where you have been for the last week. We need to send you home 'clean', as we call it.' He took the cup of coffee that Gary was offering him. 'I'd like to start straight away.'

'Can I go first?' said Freddy. He grabbed some food to take with him. 'I like a good natter with a psycho-whatsit.'

'You love the sound of your own voice, more like,' said Fabian.

Freddy and David went into a bedroom and closed the door behind them. Jac looked towards the television, wondering why Gary had switched it off. She was itching to hear more news.

'You all right?' said Gary.

Jac shrugged, and Gary stroked her arm.

Fabian coughed. He lurched towards the kitchen with an exaggerated limp.   'I've erm, just remembered, my ankle's playing up,' he said. 'Maybe I'll go and rest it.' He got some food and hobbled off in the direction of the second bedroom, before turning and smiling at Jac. He blew her a kiss and hopped out of sight.

Jac blushed. She had hoped that the boys hadn't noticed what was going on with Gary. Fat piggin' chance of that.

She sat on the sofa and Gary laid some food out on the coffee table.

'I need to talk to you about a couple of things,' he

said. He handed her a Danish pastry. He was obviously trying to cheer her up.

'Ok ...'

'We have information that Miss Steele has left the country. A woman matching her description, travelling under a false name, flew to America from Manchester Airport.'

'I'm glad.'

'But there are other JASMINE operatives still at large, and we can't rule out revenge attacks. We need to make sure you are safe, Jac.' He patted her on the leg. 'The plan is to move you out of London into a safe house. Just for a while.'

'That's cool,' she said.

'It's just a precaution,' said Gary.

'Where will I go?'

Gary shifted in his seat. 'Well, that's the other thing.' His forehead wrinkled into mini ridges. 'That's why I turned the telly off. I have news about your parents.'

A shockwave of heat spread across Jac's skin. But, inside, there was a big, black hole where her feelings should have been.

'Your mum and dad are in prison,' said Gary. He caressed the back of her hand with his thumb. 'They were picked up in Arizona and brought back here in secret. The information you gave to Daniel Bavington *did* reach the newspapers. But the story was immediately hushed up by the government, and the Bavington exposé released instead. As part of the cover up, your parents were locked in solitary confinement. But the good news is they're ok.'

'Where are they?'

'Scotland. Not far from Glenoustie Croft, it turns out.'

She felt a sob of relief rise from her chest. She tried to hold it down, but it wouldn't stay. A tear rolled down her cheek. 'I hope they can see the Croft from their piggin' cell window!'

Gary laughed. 'Do you want me to put the TV back on now?'

Jac nodded and obliterated the teardrop with the back of her hand.

The news reports about Flick Stryder and Julian Jones were not kind. Every corrupt case they had worked on was exposed. Photos were shown of them getting out of taxis drunk, and arguing in restaurants. Someone had taken a long lens photo of them at the detention centre in Scotland, walking around the yard in prison clothes.

They looked well, Jac thought. But the hard heart they had given her told her that their punishment served them right. They were due to go on trial for fraud, corruption and abuse of power. They would stay locked up for a very long time.

'So we need to talk about where you are going to live,' said Gary. 'And don't say you can look after yourself.'

'Maybe I could live with Fabes?'

'Fabian and his family are going to need time to put their lives back together in private. But I hope I have come up with a better option.'

Down in the street, a group of drummers riffed in celebration, the sound borne upwards by the warm air.

'I have an older sister. Valerie. She's a politics lecturer, and she lives near Oxford. She doesn't have any kids of her own. There are good schools nearby – and a great sixth form college that does a journalism course. What do you think? I've told her all about you.'

It sounded fantastic.

'She's ready to take you straight away.'

The bedroom door opened. 'Did I hear my name mentioned earlier?' said Fabian.

'Maybe,' said Jac.

'Thought so – my ears were burning.'

'Your ears are like radar,' said Jac. 'Little brown satellite dishes strapped to the sides of your face.'

'They are very handsome ears.' Fabian preened and struck a pose.

'Shame about the rest of you, then.'

Fabian clutched his heart and staggered about, pretending to be mortally wounded by Jac's comment.

'I notice your limp has gone,' she said. 'You goof.'

'That's because I've rested it.'

'Ha ha.'

There was an earth-shattering bang. The windows in the flat imploded, and huge chunks of glass flew across the room, spinning and reflecting the sunlight. The fragments hit the walls, disintegrating into splinters and shedding razor-sharp dust. For a brief moment there was silence outside, except for the wailing of car alarms. And then the screaming started.

Her ears ringing, Jac picked tiny specks of glass out of her hands.

'Probably a car bomb.' Gary went over to the window and looked out. 'It's started already.'

Freddy and David rushed into the room, brushing glass dust from their clothes and hair.

'What's started?'

'Harmony-Haters,' said Gary. People who are desperate to destroy peace.'

'You find them wherever there is a move towards order and change,' said David. 'They are very angry people. They will support any cause, just so they have an excuse to create damage and fear.'

'I'm afraid we're going to see a lot of this,' said Gary.

'Is Fabe still in the other room?' said Freddy, looking round.

'No – he came out,' said Jac.

'Where is he, then?'

'He dived behind the settee,' said Gary, moving away from the window. 'Are you all right, mate?'

There was no answer.

'Fabe?' Freddy walked round the back of the sofa. His face whitened and he reeled. David moved to catch him. Jac and Gary hurried to Fabian's side, and Jac felt huge, unstoppable tears dropping from her eyes.

Fabian was barely conscious, his skin grey.

Protruding from his neck was a shard of glass the size of a carving knife.

LX

The ambulance took ages to come.

Gary, Freddy, David and Jac took turns to press their fists into Fabian's neck, piling layer upon layer of ripped clothing and towels onto the wound. The bleeding slowed, but never stopped. The four of them whispered – urged – Fabian to stay with them and not give up the fight.

Gary wiped a smear of blood from the face of his watch and shook his head. There were sirens going off everywhere – but they all seemed to be for somebody else.

A wave of dizziness came over Jac and she staggered to the window. A thick column of black smoke cut the view in half, and the fresh air she sought smelt dirty and burnt. She thought she was going to be sick – then her stomach lurched with relief as an ambulance arrived below and two paramedics took a trolley from the back, pushed it across the pavement and into the entrance hall.

She ran into the corridor and waited for the lift to arrive. The ambulance crew followed her into the flat, and Freddy, Gary and David stood back and watched the medics get to work.

'Somebody's done a good job of stemming the

blood,' said one of the ambulance personnel. They inserted a drip into Fabian's arm, lifted him onto the stretcher and wheeled him out of the flat.

Everyone quickly agreed that David should stay behind; Jac, Freddy and Gary got into the lift with Fabian and they descended to the ground floor in silence.

By the time they had reached the ambulance all the fluid from the drip had disappeared. The paramedic bit his lip and replaced the bag.

'Only one passenger,' he said.

Freddy slipped through the ambulance door as Fabian was wheeled inside. The paramedics secured Fabian, the doors closed and the ambulance drove off.

Within moments the wailing of the siren seemed miles away.

'What do we do now?' Jac squeezed Gary's arm and tried to swallow an aching lump which had appeared in her throat.

'We follow,' said Gary. He strode to a nearby car, reached through the blown-out window and pulled a set of keys from behind the sun visor.

'Lucky guess,' he said. He unlocked the doors and they climbed in.

The streets were almost empty. Jac stared at the road through the hole where the windscreen should have been. Everywhere was covered in black dust.

'I did a terrible thing to Fabian, you know.'

'I do know. After we intercepted the death threat, we hacked your computer. But you do realise that getting Barnaby Traves sacked probably saved this country?'

'I still don't think I should have done it. I should have loved Fabes more than that.'

'You gave him the best thing you could. A safer world to live in.'

'Yeah. I told myself that at the time. But the truth is, I was being selfish and I wanted to hurt him. I don't know how he'll forgive me.'

'He's a good friend.'

'He's the most amazing friend I've ever had.' She looked at the dust on the bonnet of the car. 'You know what's funny?' she said. 'It didn't make me jealous. When Freddy got in the ambulance, I mean. I thought I'd resent it, but I didn't. Fabes needs Freddy more than he needs me.'

'That's my girl,' said Gary, and he patted her on the leg.

They turned a corner, and the ambulance was ahead of them at the next set of traffic lights. The lights went green – but the ambulance didn't move off.

'What's the matter with them?' said Jac. She cupped her hands and called out of the window. 'Get a move on, you bunch of snails!'

Gary pushed the car into a high gear and accelerated towards the lights. He swerved round the ambulance and left it behind.

'What are you doing?' yelled Jac.

Gary didn't slow the car. 'I'm making sure you don't try and get out.'

'*What?*' Jac turned to look at him.

'I'm sorry, babe.' He pushed the car harder. 'The only reason they stop an ambulance is ... if they need to resuscitate.'

'No!' A sickening mist of tiny white stars clouded Jac's vision. A whining noise penetrated her ears and nothing felt real. She felt the car hurtle onwards, finally veering into the hospital car park and jolting to a halt.   She stumbled into the Accident and Emergency waiting room with Gary at her side. They waited in silence.

There was no news for over an hour.

LXI

It was dark outside: the clocks had gone back a week ago and the nights were getting colder.

Jac hadn't seen Gary for three months. He was undercover somewhere in Asia; that was all she knew. Back in July, God's Profiteers had disappeared – and so had all their money. Gary was working with the Black Rats' sister organisation, the Lucky Dragons, trying to locate the Profiteers' bank accounts and bring them to justice.

She got into bed, and as she drew the duvet around her chest, her laptop let out a series of beeps. Someone was video-calling her.

There was a knock at the bedroom door, and Valerie came in with a mug of hot chocolate.

'Hi,' said Jac.

'Don't be late going to bed,' said Valerie. 'You've got a big day tomorrow.' She put the mug on the bedside table, turned round and spoke into the laptop. 'Good night, Fabian. Make sure she gets enough beauty sleep.' She smiled and left the room.

Fabian pulled a face from a window on the screen. 'You'll never get enough of *that*.'

'Shut your gob.' Jac took a mouthful of chocolate, squeezed it into her cheeks and leered back at him.

'That's much better,' he said.

He looked thinner – and older. Losing six pints of blood and needing two transfusions was enough to make anyone grow up quickly. Jac looked at the scar on his neck as they talked: four centimetres across, still angry and pink, and raw with trauma.

In the intensive care unit, Jac had never cried so much in her life. Fabian had been on the critical list for two days. Freddy had sat by his bed the whole time, moving only to take little Jonas to the café or toilets, whilst Fabian's parents kept vigil.

But Fabian had come through ... and was now being an attention-seeking goof and talking about himself, as usual.

'Rufus came to visit me yesterday. Brought me some CD's.'

'Piggin' heck! It was nice of him, though.'

'I told him to bum off – and he told me I was a gay-boy nerd.' He showed Jac one of the CD's. 'I guess that means we're friends.' He smiled. 'He said sorry, too.'

'So when do you think you'll go back to school?'

'A couple of weeks.'

'How's Freddy?'

'He's just about keeping his probation officer happy. And he got the lead role at drama club ... and has been annoying me ever since, practising his lines.'

'Does he still visit you every day?'

'Yeah. He's brilliant, isn't he?' The grown-up, hardened look in his eyes disappeared, and for a moment they twinkled. 'Hey, guess what? My dad's got a new job.'

'That's really good.' Jac's conscience pricked her, despite Fabian's smile.

'Some sort of goodwill ambassador to Europe,' Fabian continued. 'He's going to Italy next week, helping them start up new businesses. And then he's off to France.'

Jac thought of Colette's deserted house in Grimaud and changed the subject. 'I got a text from Gary two nights ago.' It had been the first one in three weeks.

'How is he?'

'Fine.'

'And he loves you?'

'Yes ...' She watched her cheeks glow pink in the video picture on the the screen.

'Is he still fighting the Anti-Harmony groups in Wales?'

'Yes,' she lied.

'And I suppose you can't tell me if you are involved in any of that.'

'I don't know what you mean!' Her heart quickened. Since August she had been sending and receiving secret messages for the Black Rats, fighting for freedom against the Harmony-Haters.

'What time's your interview tomorrow?' said Fabian.

'Two thirty. They're letting me out of school early.'

Valerie had a friend who worked at the local newspaper, and had put Jac forward for a work experience scheme.

'I won't sleep!' said Jac. 'I'll be the youngest person to do it if they say yes.'

'Which they will ...'

The distant sound of a doorbell distracted Fabian for a moment. Not long afterwards his bedroom door opened and Freddy came in. He waved at Jac cheerfully.

'Watcha,' said Jac.

'I got you this.' Freddy gave Fabian an enormous toy gorilla wearing a baseball cap. 'To cheer you up. Your mum says I can't stay, though.'

To Jac's amusement Fabian looked genuinely pleased with it. 'It's got a face like a bulldog!' she said. 'And it's boss-eyed.'

'Must be your sister,' said Fabian.

'Ha piggin' ha,' said Jac. 'Look, I should go.'

'*Au revoir, petit pois,*' said Freddy. 'Good luck.'

'*Courage and comfort. All shall yet go well.* Nighty-night!' Fabian blew her a kiss. 'You look nice by the way ... have you got make-up on?'

'Shut up,' said Jac. She terminated the call.

She closed the laptop and opened a drawer on her bedside table. She took out some make-up remover and cotton wool pads. With deft movements she removed the last traces of black mascara and kohl eyeliner. Using another pad, she wiped off a trace of soft pink blusher.

At the back of the drawer was a pile of prison visiting orders. Every week, her parents had asked her to go and see them. She had refused. She took a bottle of moisturiser and massaged it into her skin. Patting her cheeks, she turned her back on the bundle of documents and pushed her parents out of her mind.

She hung up her dressing gown and returned to the bed, unclasping the glass bead necklace that Gary had given her. She pressed it to her lips and, clutching it tightly, slipped under the duvet and tried to get some sleep.

LXII

As Jac ate her breakfast the next morning there was a knock at the door.

'Can you get that?' called Valerie.

Jac walked down the hallway, chewing on a piece of toast and marmite. She pulled open the door, ready to crack a joke about it being too early for visitors.

But the words she had prepared were blown out of her head. She swooned and dropped her toast. The street outside seemed to fold in and suffocate her, and she thought she was going to throw up. She tried to keep her eyes open, but she was losing consciousness fast.

What had she just seen? Surely it was a dream.

But it was real: standing on the doorstep, with a big bunch of flowers, was Colette.

The floor came up to meet her and she hit it with a bang.

LXIII

'I am so sorry.' Colette clasped Jac's hand in both of hers.

Valerie handed Jac a mug of tea and she sipped it slowly.

'I've phoned the school,' said Valerie. 'They said you should take tomorrow off as well, given the circumstances. Do you want me to phone the newspaper and cancel your interview?'

'No,' said Jac. 'I still want to go ... if Colette doesn't mind?'

'You must go!' said Colette. 'I slept badly at the hotel in London. I will rest here while you are out.'

Valerie looked at her watch. 'I have to leave. Help yourself to breakfast, Colette – Jac will show you where everything is.' She pulled on her jacket and hurried out of the house.

'Thanks, Val.' Jac turned to look at Colette again, hardly daring to believe she was real. She put her hand to her neck and touched the necklace Gary had given her, wishing she could tell him what had happened. Colette noticed the glass beads and looked upset.

'Oh, my friend ... the beautiful bracelet you gave me. I am afraid I do not have it. We sold it in exchange for petrol and food. It completely broke my heart, but ...'

'It's fine,' said Jac. 'I saw what it was like in France. You had to do it.' She tore off a sheet of kitchen paper and handed it to Colette so she could wipe her eyes. 'So, what happened to you?'

Colette blew her nose. 'Grimaud had become a bad place to live. Then we heard of a community in the countryside near Grenoble. They were growing their own food and living without stealing and fighting. We needed petrol to drive four hundred kilometres. So we sold everything to pay for it, and we went. And it was ok there.'

'You weren't scared?'

'There were rumours of a terrible army who wanted to make us slaves. But they never came. Sometimes there were big explosions in the mountains, but no nearer. Then one day, a man arrived in our camp. He told us that the army had been stopped and that perhaps our lives would return to normal again. He stayed with us for two days, and before he left, he did the strangest thing.'

Jac waited for Colette to blow her nose again.

'He came to our hut and asked to speak to me. He gave me a train ticket to England, and a hotel booking – so expensive! And ... your address. Well – we didn't even know the trains were running, so that was a big surprise. But then he gave me ...' She went out into the hall and Jac heard her unzip her bag. 'It is a letter. A letter for you.'

Jac turned the envelope over in her hands. Her name was scrawled over it, as if written in a hurry.

'What did he look like? The man who gave this to you?'

'Short. But strong ... and golden hair.'

It wasn't Jean-Luc.
Jac pulled the letter open and began to read.

TO MADEMOISELLE JAC

JEAN-LUC CHAPUT DIED IN
AUGUST.
HE WAS FIGHTING AN ARMY OF
UNSPEAKABLE EVIL IN THE FRENCH
ALPS. IT WAS HIS LAST WISH THAT
YOU SHOULD HEAR THESE WORDS:

'Jac. You are a strong, stubborn
girl. I knew that if I lied to you
about your friend, it would put
fire in your heart. It would make
you determined to put things
right.
Unfortunately, the lie hurt
you - and I am sorry.

But I do not regret it.

See what great things you
achieved? Sometimes we need
pain to make us act.
That is important to remember.

Farewell. Jean-Luc.'

THANK YOU. YOURS SINCERELY ...

266

The signature at the bottom was smudged.

'Are you ok?' Colette looked at her anxiously.

Jac threw the letter on the floor.

'Perhaps, another drink of tea?' said Colette.

'Thanks.' Jac's head was spinning with rage. How dare he do that to her? Jean-Luc had used her. From the very moment she had insisted on travelling to Grimaud to look for Colette, he must have decided to manipulate her. She remembered the fire in his eyes when he said he would to take her to Colette's house after all. She could see now that he was preparing a web of lies to provoke her into action. He couldn't have believed his luck when he saw that Colette's family had abandoned their home! But Jac knew Jean-Luc was right. She would never have done any of it if she had believed that Colette was alive.

But she would never forgive him.

She folded the letter in half, got up and followed Colette into the kitchen.

'When's the last time you made a video call?'

'I haven't even listened to the radio for nine months.'

'Well, there's someone I want you to meet!'

They went to her bedroom and Jac switched on her laptop. She and Colette sat on the bed and they positioned the computer so they were both in the video frame. Jac used the touchpad to activate the 'call' button, and the ring tone beeped from the screen.

Fabes was going to be blown away by this.

LXIV

Jac stood with Colette by the Eurostar ticket barrier at St Pancras International station. They hugged.

'I have had such a wonderful two weeks! Thank you!' Colette searched in her bag for her ticket and looked at the departure boards. 'I must go. Good luck with your job at the newspaper. And thank you for these wonderful presents.' She patted her new suitcase, packed with clothes for her family.

'There's some chocolate in there, too,' said Jac. 'And, before you go: just one more gift.'

She took a small bag out of her pocket and pressed it into Colette's hand. Colette opened it; inside was a bracelet made of hand-carved, wooden beads.

'It's beautiful.' Colette looked as if she might cry. 'And I promise, I will never ...'

'Hey! You can do what you like with it! And I'll come and visit soon.'

They hugged again, and Colette walked to the barrier. The machine drew in her ticket and spat it out again, and the gate opened. She waved goodbye to Jac and went to passport control.

Jac watched her go, then strode across the concourse to find a coffee shop. Her heart fluttered as she wove between people and their luggage. Yellow-white rays from the autumn sun filtered through the station roof, glinting on the filigree of metal frames that held the glass. She bought a newspaper; Richard Masters was on the front page, announcing that attacks by the Harmony Haters had been reduced by sixty per cent. The paper also reported rumours that God's Profiteers' bank accounts had been located and frozen. It said that it was only a matter of time before the leaders of the Profiteers were discovered and brought to justice.

She found a corner seat in a cake shop and ordered a slice of chocolate gateau with cream. Whilst she waited for it to arrive she got out her phone and re-read the text she had received the day before.

Home tomorrow. Eurostar 15.00 G x

Her heart danced and she knew she was smiling.

She hugged her cup of coffee and looked up at the golden-edged station clock.

She only had two hours to wait.

THE END

Acknowledgements

Louise Voss, for continued support, constructive editing and inspiring feedback. Sheila Holdsworth and Sue Aston for support above and beyond the call of duty. Emily Cook and everyone at Khushi Feet for the privilege of helping to promote such a wonderful charity. Eleanor North and Julie Collins-Wood for help with French translation. Penny Ewles-Bergeron for information about life in the South of France. And to all my wonderful family and friends: thank you for everything.

Want more adventure, friendship and fun?

Go to **www.fionabeddowbooks.com** for news, articles, interviews and writer's secrets.

Fiona Beddow is on Twitter : **@FionaBeddow**

The JASMINE Portfolio and Fiona Beddow's first novel Fierce Resistance have a Facebook page! **facebook.com/FionaBeddowBooks**

WHAT'S NEXT?

Another moving and gripping story about an adventurous girl is on its way!

check out
www.fionabeddowbooks.com
and
Facebook.com/FionaBeddowBooks
for updates

Printed in Great Britain
by Amazon.co.uk, Ltd.,
Marston Gate.